SEPTIMUS HEAP

The Magykal Papers

ALSO BY ANGIE SAGE

Septimus Heap, Book One: **Magyk**

Septimus Heap, Book Two: **Flyte**

Septimus Heap, Book Three: **Physik**

Septimus Heap, Book Four: **Queste**

Araminta Spookie: **My Haunted House**

Araminta Spookie: **The Sword in the Grotto**

Araminta Spookie: **Frognapped**

Araminta Spookie: **Vampire Brat**

Araminta Spookie: **Ghostsitters**

SEPTIMUS HEAP

The Magykal Papers

ANGIE SAGE

ILLUSTRATIONS BY MARK ZUG

KATHERINE TEGEN BOOKS

An Imprint of HarperCollinsPublishers

To my uncle and aunt, Charles and Anna, with love

—A.S.

For Janelle

—M.Z.

The artist would like to thank Janelle Bender for her doodles
in the hand of Jenna Heap and Lucy Gringe.

Portraits in the Pigeon Post Biography series were rendered by Max Zatzuma.

Septimus Heap is a trademark of HarperCollins Publishers.

Septimus Heap: The Magykal Papers
Text copyright © 2009 by Angie Sage
Illustrations copyright © 2005, 2006, 2008, 2009 by Mark Zug

www.harpercollinschildrens.com

Library of Congress Cataloging-in-Publication Data
Sage, Angie.
 The Magykal papers / Angie Sage ; illustrations by Mark Zug. — 1st ed.
  p. cm. — (Septimus Heap)
 Summary: Purports to be a compilation of pamphlets, journals, restaurant reviews,
maps, historical information, and other never-before-published papers from the world of
the apprentice wizard Septimus Heap.
 ISBN 978-0-06-170416-1 (trade bdg.)
 [1. Fantasy.] I. Zug, Mark, ill. II. Title.
PZ7.S13035Mb 2009   2008027110
[Fic]—dc22   CIP
                                                                         AC

Typography by Robert Brook Allen
18 19 20 LEO 10 9 8 7 6
❖
First Edition

A NOTE FROM

The Editors

In this volume, you will find a collection of papers that will augment your knowledge of the Castle where the Heap family dwells, as well as papers from the Wizard Tower and the Palace. Many of these are excerpts from previously published works, such as the Pigeon Post Biography series, the Heaps of History series, and other popular pamphlets that have been widely distributed. You will also find some useful flyers and listings for popular destinations and restaurants as well as helpful maps.

Much of the material here, however, has never been published before, such as the private journals of Jenna Heap, Marcia Overstrand, and Septimus Heap. You will also find the secret files of the Supreme Custodian and excerpts from the journals of Stanley and fascinating dispatches from the Message Rat Office.

Read on to enter the world of

SEPTIMUS HEAP

CONTENTS

✢ PAPERS FROM ✢
THE PALACE

✢ PAPERS FROM ✢
AROUND THE CASTLE

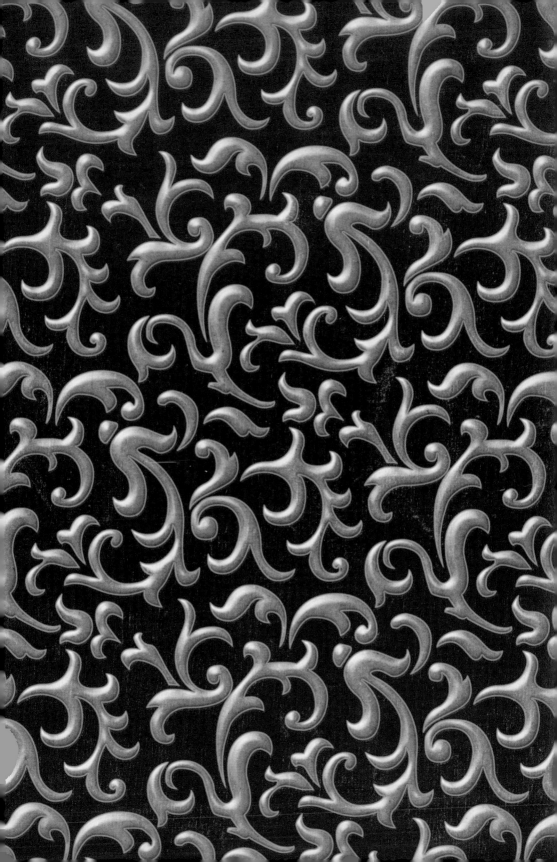

⊹ PAPERS FROM ⊹

THE CASTLE

A HISTORY OF THE CASTLE

LONG, LONG AGO, BEFORE THE TIME OF HOTEP-RA, before even the first Queen arrived on her Royal Barge, a small village was nestled beside a river bend.

The village had begun its life as a place of refuge for those escaping from the nearby Forest, which was a Darke and dangerous place. The villagers were quiet people and wanted no trouble. They dug a ditch between themselves and the Forest and put up a long, low dry-stone wall beside it; they tended their crops and their livestock and kept to themselves. The village traded with the Port and with the Farmlands; it prospered and grew, and the ditch and the wall crept out toward the Forest.

But the prosperity of the village came to the attention of the Forest creatures, who wanted some of the rich pickings to be found there. At night the villagers would lock their doors and listen fearfully as werewolves, witches and all manner of **Darke Things** came in from the Forest, creeping and rustling, snuffling and snarling through the lanes. The creatures took their chickens and goats, **Blighted** the crops, **Fouled** the wells, and one stifling summer's night, they stole a baby from her crib as she lay by an open window.

The night after the baby was taken, the villagers began the Wall. For months they worked, building a strong, high wall on their side of the ditch, sealing the gaps in the stones with lime, taking it higher than anyone thought it was possible for a wall to be. It was thick too—as thick as a man was tall—and along the top ran a broad path for the newly formed Forest Night Patrol to tread. They worked through three summers and four freezing winters until at last the Wall surrounded the village and the Castle was born.

Now the villagers began to feel safe.

But *still* the occasional **Darke** Forest creatures ventured in. Climbing **Things** with suckered feet and razor-sharp teeth would creep over at night, and the occasional scream would pierce the night air as an unwary villager was caught in the light of a full moon.

The next spring, undeterred, the Castle-dwellers dug their ditch deeper and deeper. Once more they worked into the winter, stopping for the Big Freeze, starting again in the spring. Deeper and deeper they dug until brown river water began to seep in. An air of expectation filled the village.

MidSummer Day was a sacred day for the villagers, as that was the one day of the year when no Forest tree shadows fell upon their land. And so, on that particular MidSummer Day, the villagers divided into two halves—one half to each end of the ditch. At the sound of a trumpet blown from the top of the Wall they breached the banks between the ditch and the river. The water roared in, a great cheer went up and their ditch became the Moat. A Mid-Summer Day Feast was held and all the villagers slept well in their beds that night.

The North Gate gatehouse and drawbridge were built some years later, when the old wooden bridge across the river to the Farmlands collapsed in a fast and high spring tide with the loss of many lives. It was decided for safety to build two new stone bridges (one-way traffic on each) where the span was less, but the only place for this was a little way upriver, outside the Wall. The Castle-dwelllers had no intention of letting any Forest creatures back into their lives and decided on a drawbridge that would be raised at sunset and lowered at dawn.

In the end only one stone bridge was built. Castle jokers called it the One Way Bridge, and the name stuck.

ONE WAY BRIDGE

The summer before the Moat was completed, a strange thing happened. On a hot midsummer's day, under a sky of brilliant blue, a beautiful, ornately gilded barge bedecked with fluttering red canopies came up the river. It had gathered quite a crowd by the time it tied up on the long, low riverbank some way up past Raven's Rock.

The occupants of the barge were a beautiful dark-haired young woman with deep violet eyes and her three dark-haired tiny daughters. The young woman spoke a strange language that no one in the Castle had ever heard before, and she was dressed in rich red velvet edged with thick gold ribbons and—to the fascination of the crowd—she wore a *crown*.

At this time, the Castle inhabitants were still simple folk without much learning. They dressed in plain clothes woven from flax grown in the Farmlands and they knew little of gold or finery. The young Queen—for this was what they took her to be—made a huge impression. And it seemed that the Castle folk made a pretty good impression on the young Queen, for she showed no signs of wanting to leave. She and her daughters spent the long, hot summer living on their barge—as they had done for many years—and when the chill winds of autumn blew up the river the Castle folk gave her the best house in the Castle to live in.

This house was on the site of what was soon to become the Palace. It was built from the same yellow sandstone that all the Castle houses were built from in those days. Over the years the house was added to and improved upon until it grew to become the Palace—a beautiful long, low building with a turret at either end and wide lawns sweeping down to the river and the Palace Landing Stage where the Royal Barge first drew up.

The young Queen soon learned the language of the Castle and the surrounding areas, and her three daughters all grew up speaking it as their mother tongue. The Queen never did say where she came from or why she had left, and somehow no one in the Castle ever quite liked to ask her. What did it matter after all? They had their Queen, and the Queen had her Castle. It was an arrangement that suited everyone.

Many years later, when that Queen's great-great-great-great—and then some—granddaughter was Queen, another momentous arrival occurred—one that was to change the Castle forever. Hotep-Ra, the very first ExtraOrdinary Wizard, arrived.

HOTEP-RA

Hotep-Ra did not, however, arrive in quite the same style as the Queen had once done. He came, bedraggled and tired, and not a little dispirited, on the night Port barge. The weather was atrocious and Hotep-Ra had spent an uncomfortable night in the hold with some crates of overripe cheese, six terrified and very noisy piglets and some aggressive Port barge rats. He felt quite sick as he disembarked at the Quay and made his way into the Castle, which—with its slowly tolling bells and miserable-looking inhabitants—seemed to him a blighted and gloomy place.

Hotep-Ra soon found out the reason for the gloom—the adored eldest daughter of the Queen was dangerously ill. She was not expected to live to see another day. It had been a long time since Hotep-Ra had used his amazing combination of **Magyk** and **Physik** skills (he had been too much concerned with boat repairs for many years), but it was not long before he had talked his way into the Palace and was at the bedside of the Queen's daughter.

The Queen was not impressed with this stranger who professed to be able to cure her daughter. He was soaking wet, he wore a filthy old purple cloak and he smelled of pigs, but the Queen was wise enough to know that the most wonderful talent may be hidden in the oddest wrappings—and besides, she was desperate.

The Queen watched while Hotep-Ra stood very still and gazed for many long minutes at the Princess, who lay as white as the fine linen sheets that swathed her and as still as the great oak bedposts that rose all the way to the ceiling far above. And then, very slowly, Hotep-Ra leaned forward, took a deep breath in and breathed out. His breath came tumbling out in a long stream of pink mist, on and on it came, seemingly endless, enveloping the Princess. The Queen had never seen anything like it—how could anyone breathe out like that for so *long*?

And then it stopped. Hotep-Ra stepped back, exhausted. Suddenly the Princess opened her eyes, smiled and sat up. Five minutes later the Princess was eating a cheese sandwich, and Hotep-Ra was a hero.

The Queen offered Hotep-Ra anything that he wanted. All he asked for was a small plot of land in the middle of the Castle and help to build a tower. The middle of the Castle was already taken

THE BUILDING OF THE WIZARD TOWER

by a couple of Alchemists who refused to move, so Hotep-Ra settled for a very desirable spot at the end of a long, wide avenue known as the Way and within sight of the Palace. Here, to the amazement of the Castle inhabitants, he built the Wizard Tower and became the very first ExtraOrdinary Wizard.

The wonders of the Wizard Tower drew many people to the Castle, and soon the Ramblings was begun to provide the new residents with somewhere decent to live. The Ramblings was not planned—it just grew. People who needed a roof over their heads would help out until a few rooms were finished; then they would move in and others would take over. And so a huge warren of rooms and walkways began to grow along the river on the east side of the Castle. The Ramblings was soon stuffed with families and became a busy, noisy place with hundreds of little windows looking out over the river, a myriad of tiny roof gardens, theaters, shops, small factories and workshops, nurseries and schools. It was a wonderful place to live.

RUPERT GRINGE'S
AROUND-THE-CASTLE BOAT TOUR

TAKE A RIDE ON RUPERT GRINGE'S AROUND-THE-CASTLE BOAT TOUR!

Starts high tide every Saturday at Jannit Maarten's boatyard.

Early booking advisable.

Now, for the first time ever, tours of the Moat are available in Rupert Gringe's revolutionary new twin-hull boat.

Learn about the fascinating history of our Castle from on-board local historian and Moat enthusiast Sirius Weazal. **Feel** the wind in our sails as we skim the river waves. **See** the hidden nooks and crannies of the Castle Wall and the Ramblings. **Hear** stories of daring and dastardly deeds through the ages.

This amazing journey is fully endorsed by the Castle Protection Trust and the Wizard Way Conservation Society.

Take your litter home.

The Moat

Hear the history of our ancient waterway. See the haunted Outside Path. Listen to tales of the mysterious Moat Fire, the ghostly wanderings of ancient smugglers and drowned lovers.

East Gate Lookout Tower

Hear the strange story of Queen Datchet III.

Snake Slipway

Home of the Rupert pedal boats. Reputedly haunted by an ancient Alchemist. Site of recent sightings of Moat Fire.

We will tie up at the swimming platform for those who wish to use the local facilities.

The Palace Landing Stage

See the haunted Pavilion erected by our Princess at the very spot where the Chief Customs Officer of the Port saved her life.

The Palace

Marvel at one of the oldest buildings in the Castle. See its beautiful lawns and gardens.

The New Dragon Field

See the all-new dragon kennel. Marvel at the sight of the Apprentice's Dragon. *Dragon sighting not guaranteed.*

The Ramblings

See them as you have
never seen them before.
Hear tales of how they
were built from our
Ramblings resident
Sirius Weazal. There
will be a competition for
children under ten to
count the clotheslines.

Sally Mullin's Tea and Ale House

We will stop here for ale and barley cake, price included.
Sally herself will tell us the terrifying tale of the night of the
fire that burned the Tea and Ale House to the ground.

The Municipal Rubbish Dump

We will pass quickly by.

The South Gate

Gateway to the Traders' Market. Hear the secrets only
Traders know!

Haunted Landing Stage

See the tiny stone quay at the mouth
of a tunnel, reputed to be where
Queen Etheldredda tried to drown her
daughter, Esmeralda.

North Gate Gatehouse

Marvel as, by kind permission of Mr.
Augustus Gringe, the drawbridge is
raised especially for us to pass beneath.

Dragon House

See the gold plaque and the burns from Dragon's Fyre.

DON'T MISS THIS ONE-OF-A-KIND TOUR!

Lifebelts provided.

SIRIUS WEAZAL would like to draw your
attention to a proposed "Ask Sirius" Walking
Tour of the Castle and the Ramblings: a
guided walk through the highways and
byways of the Castle and the Ramblings where
you can ask Sirius anything about the Castle.
Money back **guaranteed** if Sirius cannot
answer your Castle question!

FIND OUT:

- Why Queen Datchet III moved the East
  Lookout Tower to the West
- If there are tunnels running beneath the
  Castle (and if some of them are **full of ice**)
- What really goes on in the Manuscriptorium
- How many miles of corridors there are in
  the Ramblings
- How many pairs of shoes the ExtraOrdinary
  Wizard owns
- The weight of the lapis lazuli in the Great Arch
- How many Mussmancers there are in the Castle
- The secret of the Draper Clock
- And much, **much** more!

Bookings taken now.
Sturdy shoes recommended.
Umbrellas provided if wet.

THE EGG-ON-TOAST RESTAURANT GUIDE
by G. M. Toast

⊱ EATING IN THE CASTLE ⊰

Ma Custard's Cake Stop

★★★★★

PROPRIETOR: Ma Custard.
LOCATION: In the parlor behind the All-Day-All-Night Sweet Shop.
SERVICE: Slow but worth waiting for.
SPECIALTIES: Raisin custard pie.
MENU: A variety of cakes and pies all made by Ma Custard.

WE ATE: Raisin custard pie, banana toffee cake, custard cream buns, licorice flapjacks, custard fancies, strawberry cupcakes and a small—very small, honestly—chocolate twist.
COMMENTS: Delicious. Open hours only between four and six in the afternoon. Get there early to be sure of a seat. A well-kept secret.

The Meat Pie & Sausage Cart

★★★★★

PROPRIETOR: Not surprisingly, he wishes to remain anonymous. However, THE EGG-ON-TOAST RESTAURANT GUIDE can reveal that he is the ex-dishwasher boy from Sally Mullin's café.
LOCATION: A mobile facility to be found in the less salubrious areas. Has recently been banned from Wizard Way.
SERVICE: Surly.
SPECIALTIES: Sausage-of-the-day. (My brave assistant tried one and got a cat's claw stuck between her teeth.)

MENU: Meat pies and sausages.
WE ATE: Sausage-of-the-day. My assistant ate nothing else for the following three days.
COMMENTS: Disgusting.

Café La Gringe
JUST OPENED

★☆☆☆☆

PROPRIETOR:
Mrs. Theodora Gringe.
LOCATION: Small, drafty lean-to at the side of the North Gate gatehouse.
SERVICE: Serve yourself. Three pots of stew kept warm (just) over a small fire.
SPECIALTIES: Stew.
MENU: Brown stew, dark brown stew and very dark brown stew.
WE ATE: Stew.
COMMENTS: Sharp knives are provided to cut up the stew. You will need them.

Wizard Sandwiches

★★★☆☆

PROPRIETOR: We were unable to ascertain this. THE EGG-ON-TOAST RESTAURANT GUIDE was informed that "Wizard Sandwiches does not believe in ownership."
LOCATION: First Floor, Number 44 Wizard Way. Green door with flowers next to the Perfect Pamphlet Printers.
SERVICE:
Friendly but sometimes a little confused. Used to run a cart service but is now take-out only, although will deliver. They will accept orders by Message Rat and have regular clients all along Wizard Way.
SPECIALTIES: Whole loaf sandwiches to share with a friend. Homemade ketchup.
MENU: We couldn't find one. When THE EGG-ON-TOAST RESTAURANT GUIDE asked, we were told, "Our menu is infinite, but there's no ham today."
WE ATE: Cheese and salad rolls with apple chutney. A Manuscriptorium scribe was buying a sausage sandwich, which looked very good, but my assistant refused to go near it.
COMMENTS: Good.

THE Ramblings

HOW TO GET THERE:

BY BOAT: Take the Ramblings shuttle from the South Gate to the Ramblings Piers numbers one, two or three.

BY FOOT: Signs can be found on most streets and alleys.

BY HORSE: Not advisable. There are no stable facilities at the Ramblings.

WHO LIVES THERE: All kinds: Families, Wizards, tradespeople, gardeners, frog-farmers, fortune-tellers, actors, acrobats, spies and runaways. It is full, as Queen Etheldredda would say, of all kinds of riffraff.

WHAT YOU'LL FIND THERE: Rooms, schools, factories, workshops, theaters, a small hospital, Ramblings Chapel, nurseries, shops, bakeries, in fact pretty much everything you could possibly need.

WHY YOU'D GO THERE: If you need somewhere to live, it's the best bet in the Castle; there are generally a few rooms vacant. For a visit, it's fun, full of interesting people and there are some good lodging houses and delightful roof gardens. Interesting experimental plays are performed by the Ramblings Players and the Knights on the Tiles theatrical group. Of course there are some rundown, shadier parts of the Ramblings, but why you would want to go there is your own business and the Guide would not dream of asking.

WHY YOU WOULDN'T: Best avoided at rush hour, when the passageways can be very congested.

A Ramble through the Ramblings
WALKING TOUR

AS NARRATED BY OUR GUIDE ✛ SILAS HEAP

SET DOWN VERBATIM BY MIRIAM BING,
AS PRACTICE FOR HER MANUSCRIPTORIUM
SPEEDWRITING EXAMINATION

GOOD AFTERNOON, EVERYONE. All here? Yes? Good. Ah, hello, madam, yes we are just about to go. Better late than never, ha ha. Well, now that we *are* all here I would like to draw your attention to the fact that this is the *original* Ramble through the Ramblings Walking Tour. Beware recent inferior expeditions by a certain Sirius Weazal.

It is my pleasure to introduce you to the Ramblings. The Ramblings has been built over hundreds of years to house all the people who have come to live in our lovely Castle. It may seem a little squished to any farmers among you, but those of us who live—or used to live—here love it.

So let's get started, shall we? Gather around. Yes, around *me*, madam. Thank you. No, madam, I am not the cleaner. I am a Wizard. That's what the blue robes are. Well, I don't know what you think a Wizard is *supposed* to look like, but I can assure you that I am indeed a Wizard.

Now, ladies and gentlemen, we begin our tour

here at the North Entrance to the Ramblings. This entrance, beside the North Gate, takes you straight into the Ramblings. Follow me, please.

The noise, madam? That is the Ramblings Orange Elementary School. We have seven elementary schools in the Ramblings, each named after a color of the rainbow. My own children went to the Purple School, which has a high proportion of children from **Magykal** families. Of course you all know how **Magyk** was banned under that awful regime of the Supreme Custard Tart—ho ho, just my little joke; we can laugh about it now, but it was no fun at the time.

Now we pass through this large hall, which is where the children play after school. The swings and slides are all provided by the Ramblings Play Association. Excuse me, young man, will you come down from there, please? You'll break it swinging around like that.

We shall now exit through this passageway—single file, please, as it narrows at the steps—and enter into the residential part of the Ramblings. Be careful of the rushlights, *please*. Look, boy, if you touch one of *course* it will be hot.

May we continue? Along the passageway you will see a series of doors of all shapes, size and colors. These are the rooms where the families of the Ramblings live.

We shall now ascend the steps—please take care—to the upper corridor that overlooks the river. This has been measured at very nearly three miles in length. To your right is the bright red door where my family used to live. All my children were born here, including the Apprentice to the ExtraOrdinary Wizard, Septimus Heap. Yes, that's correct, madam, the boy with the dragon. Oh really? Well I'm very sorry, but I don't think my son has much control over the dragon poo. Yes, I'm sure it was extremely distressing.

Yes, young man, of *course* you may ask a question. Yes, this is where the Princess lived. She left on her tenth birthday. Bit of a shock, actually. Can we have a look? Well, I don't see why not. I've got a key somewhere. Kept it as a memento . . . see, fits the lock perfectly . . . oh this door always did have a mind of its own . . . open, you stupid door . . . Oof!

Yes, madam, it does indeed look rather small for a large family. Yes, six boys and a girl. Well, the girl slept in that little cupboard here. Yes, it is cute. Oh my gosh, it still has the curtains Sarah made. Oh dear. Oh. I had quite forgotten. Time to move on now, oh dear, oh dear . . .

We shall now turn down here, no down *here*, madam, and take this winding passageway—take care, it slopes down rather sharply. It's a bit of a walk, but it will take us to the upper market hall, which usually has some interesting produce. No running please, young man. You don't know who you'll bump into. There could be the ExtraOrdinary Wizard around the next bend. But we hope not, ho ho!

Right, here we are. Yes, madam, the market hall always smells like this. I think it's the cheese. Now you may look around at your leisure. We'll meet at the Home Brew Ale Stall in ten minutes. No rush.

Everyone found a bargain? Good. Now we set off for the Knight on the Tiles Little Theater, taking in Mrs. Tenderfoot's delightful roof garden on the way. Follow me, please, down this corridor. No, young man, *this* one. We don't want you getting lost, do we? Well, possibly we do . . . ahem, er, you're his father, are you? Well, I suggest you keep an eye on your son, sir. Everyone, keep left please. *Left*, madam. The workshops will soon be closing and there will be a bit of a rush.

Right, now we go through this little door here. May I suggest you take a deep breath in, madam, that usually does it. Oh. Can anyone give a push? One, two, *three*—good. Now we take the high walkway to the roof terrace. Please keep to the middle, as some of the fences are not to be trusted. Yes, it is a long way down, madam. Yes, it's the river down there. It does indeed look very small *comebackfromtheedge*! Oh heavens. Would you *kindly* keep hold of your son, sir, if you wish him to survive another day?

If those of you with a head for heights would care to stop and turn around for a moment, this is a wonderful place to see the Wizard Tower. And the golden Pyramid at the top is looking very stunning today, with the sun glinting off it. The **Magykal** lights very blue today. They are often purple too, but it does depend on the kind fo **Magyk** happening in the Tower. And for those of you who are early risers, this is a wonderful place to see the sun rise over the Farmlands.

Now, we have reached the common communal roof terrace, a gem of green hidden from the rest of the world. Only the birds can see it. Yes, and dragons, madam. If you will follow me, please, we will walk through the gardens. Please *don't pick the flowers*.

Our last port of call is the Theater. Just follow me down the winding steps this way and through this green door here. Everyone here? Good. We are now inside the Knights on the Tiles Little Theater. Yes, it is dark after being outside. No, madam, I don't know why the rushlights are not lit. I would not call it a disgrace, exactly, more of an inconvenience. Your eyes will soon get used to it; there is no need whatsoever to panic. Ouch! *Oof!* What the—

Oh my goodness, it's you, Larry! Well, how was I to know you were doing a performance? Couldn't see a thing. What, that was the idea? No, we didn't want to buy tickets. Well, I am very sorry you don't have an audience, but to tell you the truth I am not surprised. Follow me now, everyone, we are very nearly at the end of our tether. No, madam, I said tour. *Tour.*

Here Miriam Bing ran out of paper.

POINTS OF INTEREST IN
THE RAMBLINGS

Bertha's Banana Bookshop
❋ *No. 3 About Turn*

Bertha's shop specializes in books with yellow covers. Recently she has branched out into books with orange covers, but stock of these is still low.

The Big Bloomer Flower Shop
❋ *3-7 Windy Way*

All the best flowers from the rooftop gardens can be found here. Cecil and Siegfried will tell you the history of each flower—in some detail. Be sure to leave enough time for your visit.

The Gothyk Grotto
❋ *13 Little Creep Cut*

A long, narrow shop stuffed with all manner of Gothyk delights. Mainly cheap trinkets and jokes, but you can also find good copies of Darke rings and Charms if you are prepared to spend a few hours in semidarkness listening to the shopkeeper—"call me Igor"—play his bizarre version of a Darke noseflute. If you want to blend in, wear black.

SARAH AND SILAS HEAP

SILAS GREW UP IN THE RAMBLINGS. His mother was the once-lovely Jenna Crackle, and his father was a talented Wizard named Benjamin Heap. Benjamin Heap was a shape-shifter—a rare and much respected talent among Wizards.

Silas was a late baby in the family and was born the seventh son, much to everyone's delight, but when Silas turned eighteen, his father bade his family a sad farewell and went into the Forest. He wanted to take his final shape: a tree. He was loath to leave Silas, who was still young, but Benjamin knew that to become a tree he needed all his strength. He dared not wait any longer. And so he wandered through the Forest until he came to the Hidden Ancient Glades and began his slow transformation.

Silas was very upset. At the time, he was Apprentice to the ExtraOrdinary Wizard Alther Mella and struggling with his studies. He felt upset that his father had left without telling him where he was going—even though Silas knew that the Ancient Glades were a well-guarded secret. Not liking to see his Apprentice so distraught, Alther gave Silas a seven-month leave to look for his father. Silas spent six of those months wandering through the Forest, but he never found the way to the Ancient Glades, where Benjamin Heap was slowly taking root. On the last day of his leave Silas returned to the Castle with the young Sarah Willow on his arm. Sarah had been studying Herbs and Healing with Galen, the Forest Physik Woman, but when she met Silas she decided she had learned quite enough and it was time to return to the Castle.

Silas and Sarah made their home in a large room in the Ramblings, and Silas went back to his Apprenticeship—but not for long.

As the children began to arrive, Silas found it harder and harder to tear himself away from family life to spend his days among the dry and dusty books in the Wizard Tower. He hated having to leave Sarah to do all the work—even though she never complained—and one day when he came home to discover he had missed both Erik and Edd's first smiles and Sam's first steps, Silas asked Alther to release him from his Apprenticeship.

Alther agreed—and not too reluctantly. He liked Silas very much; in fact, that was one of the reasons why he had chosen him to be his Apprentice, but he knew that Silas was struggling with the more advanced **Magyk** and he thought that Silas had made the right decision.

Sarah and Silas had seven sons in all, but—as everyone knows—the youngest, Septimus, was declared dead by the Midwife and carried away. On that same night, Silas found a baby girl in the snow outside the North Gate—and now everyone knows who she is too.

The day of the baby-in-the-snow's tenth birthday, the lives of the Heap family were changed forever. Sarah's children were scattered far and wide, and although she was at last reunited with her youngest son, she lost her oldest son to the **Darke** and her next four sons to the Forest.

Sarah and Silas moved into the vast, virtually empty Palace, and not long after that she lost Nicko to his Apprenticeship with Jannit Maarten. Sarah's newfound Septimus was living at the Wizard Tower under the thumb of Marcia Overstrand, and all that was left to Sarah was her much-loved adopted daughter, Jenna. Sarah felt bereft. At night she would sometimes dream that all her lost sons were with her once more. But in the morning when she awoke to the sound of Silas snoring, Sarah would gaze mournfully up at the dusty old bed canopy and would know that it was all a dream—and a hopeless one at that.

She comforted herself with the thought that at least it could not get worse—until one day it did. Nicko disappeared from the face of the earth.

And what was even worse were the rumors flying around the Castle—that Nicko was lost in Time. It was, thought Sarah, a wicked thing to say to a mother and, obviously, totally impossible. But as the months went by and Nicko did indeed seem to have vanished, Sarah began to wonder. Those were Silas and Sarah's darkest days.

Things are a little better now, as Sarah has once again seen her second-youngest son, but she still dreams of the day when all her children will be with her at the Palace. Silas tells her not to count her chickens, but Sarah likes her chickens and she counts them every day.

BENJAMIN HEAP

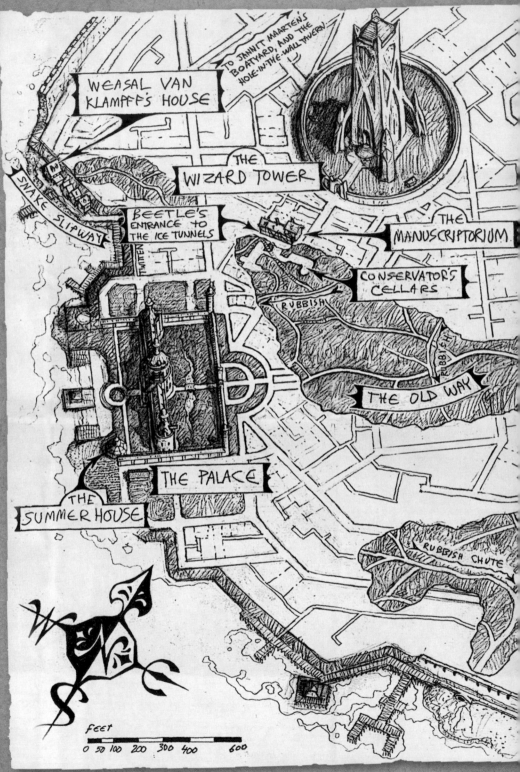

WEASAL VAN KLAMPFF'S HOUSE

TO JANNIT MAARTEN'S BOATYARD, AND THE HOLE-IN-THE-WALL TAVERN

THE WIZARD TOWER

THE MANUSCRIPTORIUM

SNAKE SLIPWAY

BEETLE'S ENTRANCE TO THE ICE TUNNELS

TWITEN

CONSERVATOR'S CELLARS

RUBBISH

RUBBISH

THE OLD WAY

THE PALACE

THE SUMMER HOUSE

RUBBISH CHUTE

feet
0 50 100 200 300 400 600

26

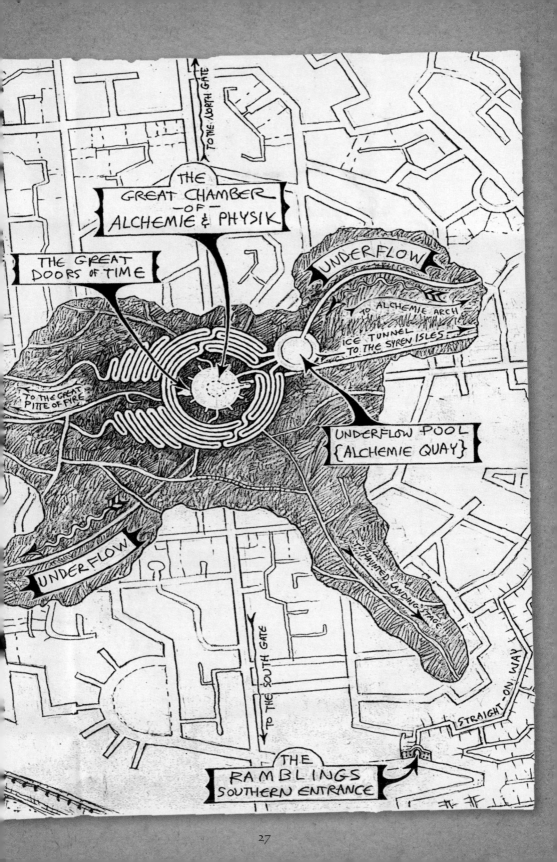

THE
GREAT CHAMBER
—OF—
ALCHEMIE & PHYSIK

THE GREAT
DOORS of TIME

TO THE NORTH GATE

UNDERFLOW

TO ALCHEMIE ARCH
ICE TUNNEL
TO THE SYREN ISLES

TO THE GREAT
PITTE OF FIRE

UNDERFLOW POOL
{ALCHEMIE QUAY}

UNDERFLOW

TO HAUNTED LANDING STAGE

TO THE SOUTH GATE

STRAIGHT-ON-WAY

THE
RAMBLINGS
SOUTHERN ENTRANCE

THE SUPREME CUSTODIAN

FTER THE ASSASSINATION of the Queen, the Supreme Custodian ruled over the Castle. He was a vicious, nasty little man, and even his mother thought he was arrogant. He was vain, much given to preening and liked wearing delicate, embroidered slippers. His hobby was lurking and listening at doors, but he never did hear anything good about himself.

His job was to find the baby Princess and get rid of her. Only then could his Master, DomDaniel, safely resume what he considered to be his rightful place at the top of the Wizard Tower as ExtraOrdinary Wizard.

The Supreme Custodian knew that once he found the Princess, his job would be at an end, so he did not try too hard—he liked the trappings of office and he particularly liked his banquets. Periodically he was summoned to see DomDaniel in the Badlands, and he would return from these visits white-faced and with a temporarily renewed vigor for the search. It was after a particularly frightening visit, where DomDaniel threatened to have him **Consumed**, that the Supreme Custodian put in a spy, Linda Lane, to check on a possible lead in Room 16, Corridor 223, East Side—a Wizard enclave in the Ramblings.

Linda Lane reported to the Supreme Custodian that the Princess—or the Queenling, as he preferred to call her—was living among the Wizards in what the house-proud Linda described as "a disgusting state of squalor." And so, on the evening of Jenna Heap's tenth birthday, the Supreme Custodian gave an Assassin her orders. But as we know, all did not go his way.

Found in the Supreme
Custodian's rooms in a
file marked HEAP

***** R E P O R T   O F *****
SENIOR SANITARY AND HOUSE CLEARANCE

OPERATIVE Nº
4

Location: Room 16, Corridor 223, East Side

Name of former residents: Heap

Value of possessions: Nil

Condition of possessions: Poor

Quantity of possessions: Seven times average amount

Books to be removed: Yes

Operative's comments: A large quantity of banned **Magyk** books were observed. Due to pressure of work I left helper to stack these outside for removal by the Book Squad. Checked later to find books had indeed been removed. Request clean uniform due to dust saturation. Book Squad later informed me that no books had been collected. Suggest investigation.

See below for list of dangerous books unaccounted for:

- Basyk **Magyk** for the Young
- **Magykal** Tales for Small Boys and Girls
- So You Think You Want to Be a Wizard?
- 101 Charms for Cleaning Houses (unused)
- **Physik** Is Bunk
- Ten Spells for Ten Smells
- Fishing Spells and Charms for Boys and Girls
- Washday Drying Spells for Busy Mothers
- How to Manage a Wizard Husband (poor condition)
- The **Magyk** of Foryx
- The Great Shape-Shifters of Our Time
- The ExtraOrdinary Apprentice Handbook

These items were removed for destruction:

- 1 Ordinary Wizard robe
- 1 bag of dried frogs
- 6 unidentified potions, possibly **Unstable**

The following decayed food was removed for composting:

- 3 turnips
- 1 pail of ? milk
- 1 brick of ? cheese
- 1 bag of Ma Custard's exploding
- 4 maggoty chickens

    rhubarb drops

These garments were sent to the Young Army Barracks:

- 10 boys' tunics, various sizes

These garments were sent to the Asylum for Distressed Persons:

- 2 girls' short tunics	condition: threadbare
- 49 odd socks	condition: disgusting
- 2 pairs of boys' boots	condition: holed

Other household items sent to the Asylum for Distressed Persons:

- 9 blankets	condition: threadbare
- 6 houseplants	condition: dead
- 8 bowls	condition: cracked
- 10 cups	condition: cracked
- 10 forks	condition: bent
- 12 spoons	condition: bent
- 5 towels	condition: threadbare
- 9 toothbrushes	condition: not nice
- 24 pens	condition: mostly broken
- 2 rubber balls	condition: chewed
- 1 mouse	condition: dead
- 1 bag of dog hair	condition: smelly

Little Theater's
WINTER SCHEDULE

The Knights on the Tiles are pleased to present
A MidWinter Feast of Festivities

Featuring:

Percy Thrower, juggling master

Recently returned from his successful tour of the Far Countries! Mr. Thrower will juggle chickens and children for the delight of all! Book early to avoid disappointment.

New Year's Eve

The Pupils of the Purple Elementary School present their annual production of the pantomime: *The Queen and Hotep-Ra*

Snow Business

A selection of short plays on the theme of snow. Audiences are requested to come dressed as snowflakes. We aim to create a blizzard!

Found in the
Heap Home

Alther Mella,
ExtraOrdinary Wizard
Wizard Tower
Wizard Way
The Castle

Dear Silas,

Thank you for your hospitality yesterday evening. It was a lovely meal. I never thought I would actually enjoy sautéed frogs; please give Sarah my thanks. I trust that little Sam has now gotten over his stomachache. It was a dramatic moment, wasn't it?

I am writing to let you know that I have reached a decision about the matters we discussed over Sarah's wonderful cream sludge pie. I have decided to agree—with some regret—to release you from your Apprenticeship.

I am extremely sad to be losing you as an Apprentice. I have enjoyed your company very much indeed, but I do understand your desire to give up your Apprenticeship and spend more time at home with your delightful—and rapidly growing—family. I do also totally understand your concerns over the DRAW at the end of the Apprenticeship. I had not meant you to find out about that quite so soon. Of course, the odds are very much against DRAWING for the QUESTE, as there is, I understand, only one stone left. But, as you say, you never know. And to leave the children without a father would be a terrible thing.

My dear Silas, please know that there will always be a seat for you at the monthly banquets, and I shall look forward to your company there. Of course, as a former Apprentice, you will receive an automatic invitation to all official functions at the Wizard Tower.

I shall be interviewing for Apprentices in a few weeks' time. There are quite a few Hopefuls to choose from. I am very impressed with that young woman Marcia, although I can see she may not be as easy to work with as you were. Good-bye to those long lunches at the Grateful Turbot, I suspect!

Thank you again for a most delightful and lively evening. With this letter you are officially Released from your Apprenticeship.

With all best wishes for the future,

Alther Mella

ExtraOrdinary Wizard

P.S. I believe I left my knife, fork and spoon with you, but don't worry, you are welcome to keep them.

Sarah Heap's Recipe for

SAUTÉED FROGS

Found in the Heap Home

PREPARATION TIME: thirty minutes; more than four hours if you have to catch the frogs first; a few days if you ask Silas to catch them

COOKING TIME: 10 to 15 minutes

One brace of frogs per person (1 brace = 2 frogs)

INGREDIENTS FOR SIX:

6 brace of frogs	1 bulb of fennel
1 chunk of butter	1 cup of flour
1 glug of cooking oil	Herbs
1 large onion	Salt and pepper to taste

SARAH SAYS: Frogs are at their best in early summer before they grow too large. You can either cultivate your own from frogspawn (see also recipe for Tadpole Soup) or find a nearby pond. I buy mine from Bertie Hatcher, who keeps the Ramblings' frog pond. His frogs are always succulent. I prepare my own, but the more squeamish can buy them ready-prepared from Bertie's stall in the Ramblings market on Saturdays.

PREPARATION:

Prepare your frogs if not already done. I recommend the method used in the *Frog-Pickers Almanac*. It is humane and not too messy.

Set prepared frogs aside.

Finely slice the onion and fennel.

Place flour in large bowl, chop the herbs and add to flour with seasoning. Mix together.

TO COOK:

Over a low fire, melt butter in heavy frying pan. Add the onion and fennel. Cook gently until the onion and fennel are soft. Remove pan from heat. Set aside the onions and fennel.

Now take the prepared frogs one by one and roll in the mixture of herbs and flour until they are coated. Set aside.

Bank up the fire. Place the frying pan over the fire; add vegetable oil and butter. When hot, add the frogs. Sauté. This will take between five and seven minutes depending on the size of the frog. Avoid overcooking, as this will lead to tough and chewy frogs.

When frogs are lightly browned, add the cooked onions and fennel, mix together for about thirty seconds, then remove from heat. Season to taste.

For a main meal, serve with fresh green beans and rice.

For an appetizer, use very small frogs and serve with a herby yogurt dip.

A great favorite in the Heap household!

Miss Match
The Purple Elementary School
The Ramblings

Dear Mr. and Mrs. Heap,

Further to your visit last week I enclose Nicko's most recent progress report.

Nicko is a very able and intelligent boy. He shows MAGYKAL potential, but, as you see, he is not making much progress. As I explained at our meeting, I do not feel that his heart is in it. He has not moved beyond the very basics and does not, as you now realize, stay behind for the MAGYKAL hour after school. I am sorry that you assumed he did. I understand he goes home via the boatyard; it appears they know him well there.

You will see from the report that Nicko excels in practical subjects. His grades for woodwork and technical design are superb.

I do understand that, as such an ancient Wizard family, you both are disappointed at Nicko's lack of interest in MAGYK, but as I said at our meeting, I think you should seriously consider allowing Nicko to take up an Apprenticeship with Jannit Maarten. I have spoken to Jannit informally about this and she would be willing to take him sometime next year.

Nicko is a very popular and valued member of this school and I would not hesitate to highly recommend him to Miss Maarten.

Yours sincerely,

Emily Match

Headmistress

WANTED

SILAS HEAP

DESCRIPTION:
Wizard. Green eyes and blond curly hair. Often disheveled. Worn robes.

LAST KNOWN WHEREABOUTS:
Seen at the North Gate by Gringe the Gatekeeper. Did not pay toll.

KNOWN ASSOCIATES:
Sarah Heap
Marcia Overstrand
Alther Mella (ghost)

SARAH HEAP

DESCRIPTION:
Blue eyes and blond curly hair. Often seen picking herbs, followed by many children. Grubby appearance.

LAST KNOWN WHEREABOUTS:
Rumored to be in the Forest.

KNOWN ASSOCIATES:
Silas Heap
Galen the Physik Woman
Sally Mullin

WANTED

By Order of the Supreme Custodian

SIMON HEAP

DESCRIPTION:
Young man with green eyes and blond curly hair.

LAST KNOWN WHEREABOUTS:
Room 16
Corridor 223
East Side

KNOWN ASSOCIATES:
Lucy Gringe

NICKO HEAP

DESCRIPTION:
Age twelve. Green eyes with blond curly hair. Dirty-looking.

LAST KNOWN WHEREABOUTS:
Seen on a boat heading downriver.

KNOWN ASSOCIATES:
Rupert Gringe
Jannit Maarten

WANTED

By Order of the Supreme Custodian

JENNA HEAP

DESCRIPTION:
Age ten. Small for her
age. Long, dark hair
and violet eyes.

LAST KNOWN WHEREABOUTS:
Seen on a boat
heading downriver.

KNOWN ASSOCIATES:
Bo Tenderfoot
Alther Mella (ghost)

YOUNG ARMY EXPENDABLE
BOY 412

DESCRIPTION:
Green eyes.
Pinched face.

LAST KNOWN WHEREABOUTS:
Seen on a boat headed
downriver. Presumed
abducted.

KNOWN ASSOCIATES:
None

SAM, EDD, ERIK AND JO-JO HEAP

DESCRIPTION:
Teenage boys. Jo-Jo Heap age fourteen. Edd and Erik Heap, identical twins age fifteen. Sam Heap age seventeen. All have green eyes and blond curly hair. Generally scruffy.

LAST KNOWN WHEREABOUTS:
Room 16
Corridor 223
East Side

KNOWN ASSOCIATES:
Silas Heap

MAXIE HEAP

DESCRIPTION:
Wolfhound. Moth-eaten.

LAST KNOWN WHEREABOUTS:
Seen on a boat heading downriver.

KNOWN ASSOCIATES:
Silas Heap
Nicko Heap

ᵗHE HEAP
FAMILY TREE

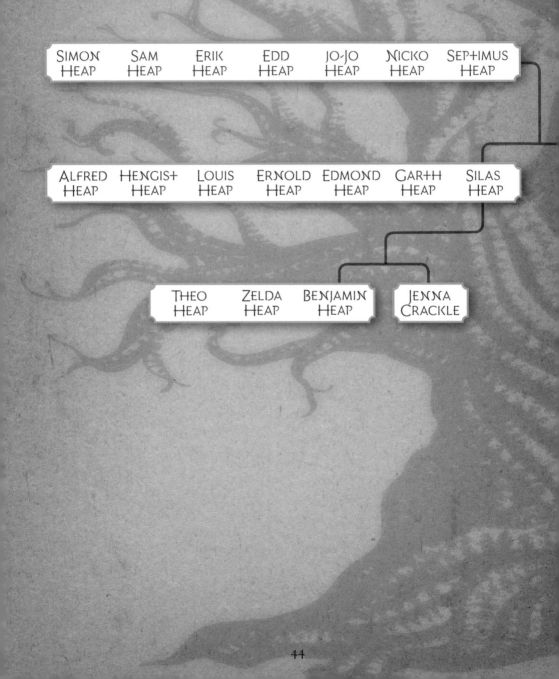

SIMON HEAP · SAM HEAP · ERIK HEAP · EDD HEAP · JO-JO HEAP · NICKO HEAP · SEPTIMUS HEAP

ALFRED HEAP · HENGIST HEAP · LOUIS HEAP · ERNOLD HEAP · EDMOND HEAP · GARTH HEAP · SILAS HEAP

THEO HEAP · ZELDA HEAP · BENJAMIN HEAP · JENNA CRACKLE

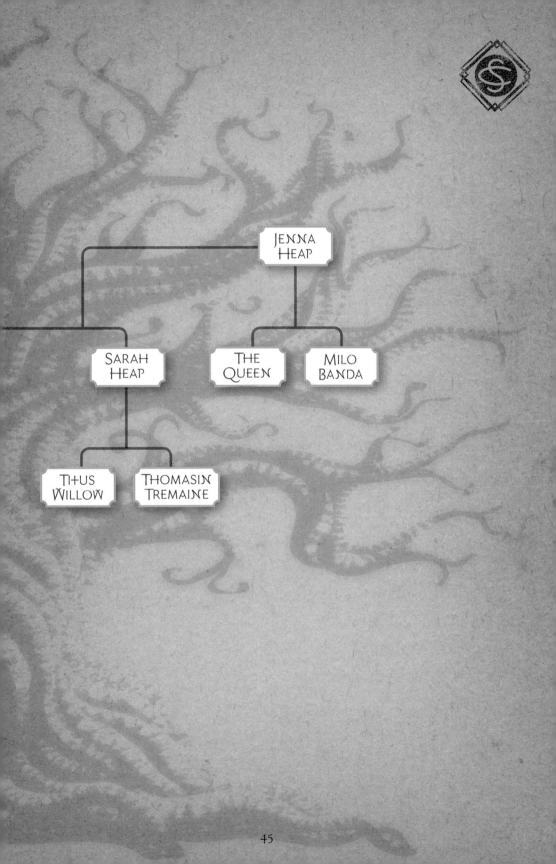

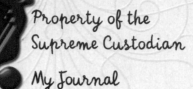

Property of the Supreme Custodian

My Journal

7:00 P.M. MONDAY

My feet are freezing. This Palace is a miserable dump. Every winter I forget how awful the Big Freeze is. Only ray of sunshine in my life is young Simon Heap. He's not a bad lad to talk to. Silly boy. Why he wants to be loyal to a bunch of useless Wizards, I have no idea, but I have a feeling it won't be for too much longer. I am definitely getting somewhere. Indeed, it is high time I got over to the Ladies' Washroom to see how he's getting on. I'll bring him one of those pies I had for lunch.

10:00 P.M. MONDAY

There was frost in the washroom; blasted fire has gone out and no coal left. But we had a nice chat, and young Heap ate the pie. He is mellowing. A week ago he wouldn't have touched it. I think he will tell me what I need to know any day now. Felt sorry leaving him alone. Would have offered him a blanket but wasn't quite sure how I could explain that to DD if he found out. Young Heap very morose. It can't be too comfortable chained to a freezing-cold radiator.

5:00 P.M. TUESDAY

Oh I feel quite ill. This afternoon got summoned by DD to the Wizard Tower. Had to walk all the way up to the top, as the stairs have ground to a halt, clogged up with a plague of DARKE cockroaches coated in Magog slime. Whole place smells disgusting and is, frankly, quite creepy nowadays with all that DARKE stuff flitting around and that ghastly wailing all the time. Say what you like about old Overstrand (and many people do), but at least she kept the Wizard Tower running properly and it smelled nice.

Of course the old toad refused to believe I am doing my best to get the information out of young Heap. I told him you catch more flies with honey, and he just laughed and said he catches flies with a flyswatter and I should try that with young Heap. Then one of those awful Magogs slid up to me, clicking its claws and breathing down my neck, while DD said that if I don't get the whereabouts of the Queenling soon he'll have me CONSUMED. Told me exactly how he would do it. Twice. I feel sick thinking about it. Oh no, another knock on the door. I feel quite weak.

6:00 P.M. TUESDAY

Thank goodness it wasn't another summons to the Tower—it was Gerald. I do enjoy calling him Gerald. He hates it, of course. "I am the *Hunter*," he said, very sniffily. Gerald gets on my nerves. He breezes in and stomps around like he owns the place. You'd never know that *he's* the one who lost the Trail, that he can't even track a bunch of smelly Wizards. Ha! I am surrounded by fools. I shall go and see young Heap again. I have a little plan, which I think might work. I am slowly bringing him to his senses through my charm and charisma. Mother was not right about *that*. I have great personal magnetism. I can see it in the way people avoid looking at me. It is all just *too* much for them.

1:00 A.M. WEDNESDAY

It has been an interesting evening. I took a nice hot drink of chocolate along with me to the Ladies' Washroom, and young Heap and I had our little chat. It was freezing, but I was fine, as I took my nice new ermine stole with me. Heap's teeth chattered, but I resisted lighting the fire—I just thought, flyswatter, flyswatter. Anyway,

I played my trump card—I "offered" Heap the possibility of an Apprenticeship to our new ExtraOrdinary Wizard. Of course, he doesn't know it's not mine to offer, but that is beside the point. It worked. He told me the Queenling has gone to stay with her aunt in the Marram Marshes. I went straight around to the barracks to see Gerald. Gerald not pleased at being woken. Said the information was of no use to him at all. But I suspected something. I am no fool, whatever Mother may say. I waited outside Gerald's window and I saw him get out his maps of the Marshes. Ha! I know what he's up to—he's going to take the credit himself. I'll go and see DD first thing tomorrow and I'll scrap that little plan. Oh yes.

10:00 A.M. WEDNESDAY

Just returned from the Wizard Tower. Got there as soon as I could, but it takes so long to dress in the mornings. I do think appearance is so important, and especially when striding purposefully along Wizard Way one has to create a good impression. As it turned out, it's a good thing I was a little late. Gerald had gotten there first and I heard all about it from that peaky-looking Apprentice that DD keeps out on the landing. DD threw Gerald out! Literally! Called him a bumbling fool and much worse. Oh joy. This has quite made my day.

2:00 A.M. THURSDAY

My nerves will not take any more. Summoned to the Wizard Tower at midnight. Was convinced I was going to be CONSUMED. But all the disgusting old fraud wanted to do was to show me some tacky blue amulet thing around his fat, sweaty neck. Got it off old Overstrand apparently. Well, good for him, although I can't say that it suits him; he looks better in black. Anyway, that at least means my plan has worked—at last—and she's in Dungeon

Number One now. Rather her than me. I left feeling a little more secure about the CONSUMED threat, but until we get the Message Rat I will not rest easy.

SATURDAY

Well, well, they've got the rat. Rat has been taken away for questioning, but seeing as it has had its Confidential status withdrawn that should not be a problem.

SUNDAY

Wretched rat proving difficult. Have had it shoved in a cage and put under the floor. It will come to its senses soon enough—I hope. Am very jumpy today. Locked myself in the bathroom in case DD's guards came for me.

MONDAY

Gerald looking very smug. Came up and whispered that he doesn't need any kind of rat—Heap or otherwise—he *knows* where the old witch is and as soon as the thaw sets in they'll be off. When I asked him which old witch, he just smiled and tapped the side of his nose in his usual I-know-something-that-you-don't kind of way. Just like all the kids used to do when I was at school . . . except I showed *them.* Now I know everything.

2:00 P.M. WEDNESDAY

Ungrateful little tick has gone! Escaped. Found the door wide open. Should never have unchained him; I am far too nice for my own good. Mother always said that—no, actually, come to think of it, Mother never did say I was too nice . . . Have set the guards after him. He'll regret this.

LINDA LANE

LINDA LANE was born in the Port. She was an only child and her parents moved to the Castle when she was seven. They found a couple of rooms in the Ramblings near the rooftop gardens and sent Linda to the Orange Elementary School.

Linda was a pretty child with long blond hair and blue eyes. She easily made friends, but she did not keep them. She would quickly make a best friend, and then as soon as she had found out all her friend's secrets, she would dump her and move on to another friend, who became the recipient for those secrets—and in return told her own. Linda worked her way around the class in this fashion until at last everyone realized what was going on. And that was the end of any friends for Linda Lane.

Linda became a lonely child. She had nothing to do but hang around trying to overhear conversations. She even got into the habit of doing that with her family, and one day she caused her own mother to be arrested and thrown into a dungeon. Linda had overheard a disparaging remark that her mother had whispered to her father about the Supreme Custodian. Linda was by then a keen member of the Custodian Youth, who met in the Palace stables every week. At Tell-Tale-Time Linda proudly related what she had heard. She won a much-coveted Tell-Tale badge and when she got home that night her mother was gone. Her father saw the badge and guessed what had happened, but he was too scared to confront his own daughter.

Linda's father was relieved when she moved out. She did not tell him that she had been recruited into the spy network and given her own rooms in the Ramblings, but he guessed that something of the sort had happened. Linda's father finally got his wife out of the dungeon by selling everything he had. They fled to the Port and never saw Linda again.

Linda was a successful spy. And when some gossip about how the Heaps' daughter looked very unlike Silas Heap reached her ears, she went with her information to the Supreme Custodian. She immediately was given a room along the corridor from the Heaps and also a crash course in herbs and healing so that she could gain Sarah's confidence. Linda soon inveigled her way into the Heap household. She put her drawing skills to use and sketched all the children and sent copies of the sketches to the Supreme Custodian. And when she discovered Jenna's date of birth, she went triumphantly to him with the news. He was convinced that Jenna was the lost Princess and the trap was set.

For her own protection and as a reward for finding the Princess, Linda was given a new name and some of the best rooms in the Ramblings, overlooking the river. But she did not enjoy them for long. Some months later she was recognized by one of her past victims, and one night as she sat drinking the very pleasant wine that the Supreme Custodian had sent over, she was pushed off her balcony and into the river, where she drowned.

Linda Lane was not seen again until the night she **Appeared** on the ghostly barge of Queen Etheldredda, where once again she proved useful to someone who was after Jenna.

A Message from Madam Marcia Overstrand, ExtraOrdinary Wizard

TO ALL IN THE CASTLE
The reign of the Supreme Custodian is over!
The Wizard Tower is back in operation,
and most of the Wizards have been Returned.
The young Princess has taken her rightful place
in the Palace with her adoptive parents,
Sarah and Silas Heap. We ask that you respect
their privacy as they become used to their new life.

The Palace Guard has been disbanded.
The Young Army has been disbanded.
All boys and girls who have lost touch with their families
have been settled into the old barracks in family groups,
for which we seek caring houseparents.
We also seek high-quality Apprenticeships
throughout the Castle.
Many people of the Castle have spent the past ten years
working for the Supreme Custodian, performing tasks
that perhaps, now, they are not so proud of.
To that end, we are happy to announce the
Second-Chance Scheme, the first of which will be
many new programs to get the Castle back on track.
Anyone may come to see us at any time and will be given
new training toward a new profession, *no questions asked*.

We do not care what you have done in the past,
only what you can do to contribute to
a brighter, better future.

✛ PAPERS FROM ✛

THE WIZARD TOWER

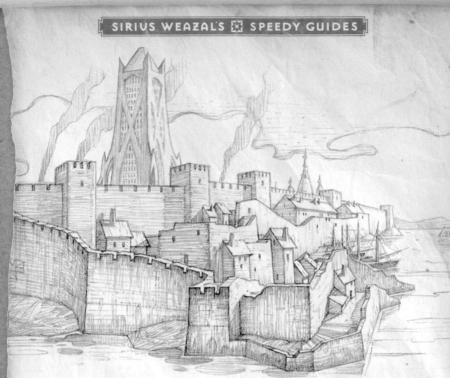

ᴛʜᴇ Wizard Tower

HOW TO GET THERE: From the Palace follow Wizard Way. Go through the Great Arch and stop for a moment to admire the amazing lapis lazuli facings. Now you are in the Wizard Tower courtyard. Cross the courtyard, ascend the marble steps and wait until the duty Wizard answers. *Do not bang on the door.*

WHO LIVES THERE: The ExtraOrdinary Wizard, the ExtraOrdinary Apprentice, Ordinary Wizards with some of their Apprentices and assorted peripheral staff.

WHY YOU'D GO THERE: You wouldn't, unless you were invited to see a Wizard.

WHY YOU WOULDN'T: Marcia Overstrand does not like unexpected visitors.

THE
Wizard Tower

NO. 3 IN THE POPULAR SERIES ✠ HEAPS OF KNOWLEDGE

A PAMPHLET BY SILAS HEAP

OTHER PAMPHLETS AVAILABLE:
HEAPS OF FUN, HEAPS OF MAGYK, HEAPS OF HANDY HINTS, HEAPS OF HERBS

DESIGNED AND BUILT by the first ExtraOrdinary Wizard, Hotep-Ra, the Wizard Tower is the Wonder of the Castle— twenty-one stories high and topped by the great golden Pyramid that houses the famous Pyramid Library, which has been collected by ExtraOrdinary Wizards across the centuries. At the very top of the Pyramid is a small, flat square inlaid with silver, on which are inscribed the unknown hieroglyphs. Tradition has it that these hieroglyphs can only be

deciphered at a time of Great Peril. A copy of a tracing of these is available at the Manuscriptorium for a considerable sum.

No one has ever been able to count the windows of the Tower and get the same number twice; this may be because of the UnStable window on the seventh floor, which is not always visible. The windows have a purple Magykal film floating over the glass, which may appear rainbow colored on a sunny day.

The Magykal lights that flicker around the Tower vary in color from light purple to dark indigo blue, depending on the amount of Magykal activity within the Tower. The underlying color of the Tower is silver.

The most dramatic approach to the Wizard Tower is along Wizard Way and through the magnificent Great Arch. As you walk across the cobbled courtyard you will see the great white marble steps leading up to the awe-inspiring double silver doors that are the entrance to the Wizard Tower. Please note this entrance is by password only.

Marcia Overstrand's apartment

The current ExtraOrdinary Wizard is Madam Marcia Overstrand. Like all ExtraOrdinary Wizards, her rooms occupy the twentieth and twenty-first floors. Madam Overstrand shares her quarters with the current ExtraOrdinary Apprentice, Master Septimus Heap—a very talented boy who is rarely allowed to leave the Tower to visit his family. However, it is tradition that the younger Apprentices live in the Tower with their Tutor Wizards. Adult Apprentices may live elsewhere if they so wish.

Dragon launchpad

Below the twentieth floor, there are generally two apartments on each floor, although on the lower stories there are some single rooms for the very junior Wizards. Wizards move up the Tower according to aptitude and experience, although some of those on the lower floors will dispute this.

FEATURES
TO NOTE

🐚 The smell of **Magyk**. Please be advised that those with allergies may be adversely affected.

🐚 The Great Hall with its **Magykal** floor. Stop awhile. If you are lucky, you will see a message cross its strangely sandy surface.

🐚 The **Magykal** silver spiral stairs. Accompanied timed rides are available on alternate Monday afternoons. Please ask the DoorKeeper for a ticket.

🐚 The **Magykal** pictures on the walls. These appear and disappear according to an ancient and long-lost Spell. The pictures depict moments from the history of the Wizard Tower. Please note that particular pictures cannot be produced on demand.

🐚 The great purple door to the ExtraOrdinary Wizard's rooms. This may be viewed as part of the spiral stairs ride. Visitors must remain silent while on the landing outside the door. You may *not* touch the door.

🐚 The fabled Pyramid Library at the top of the Tower. It is regretted that Library visits are no longer available to the public.

NOTABLE EXTRAORDINARY WIZARDS THROUGHOUT HISTORY

FIRST: HOTEP-RA

Arrived thousands of years ago from the Far Countries. Hotep-Ra built the Wizard Tower and founded the entire system of **Magyk** in the Castle. There are many legends surrounding Hotep-Ra, but most are confidential and we will not attempt to delve into them.

TALLEST: TERRENCE BROWN

Seven feet, five inches. Had all the doorframes raised in the Extra-Ordinary Wizard apartment. He suffered badly from vertigo, as many of the more talented ExtraOrdinary Wizards do.

SHORTEST: LOUANNA MOON

Four feet tall and proud of it.

YOUNGEST-SERVING: DAN FORREST

Dan Forrest was only sixteen years old when he became ExtraOrdinary Wizard. He was one of the early ExtraOrdinary Wizards, and in those times it was not so unusual for those in their teens to hold important positions, because people tended not to live so long.

Dan was a popular ExtraOrdinary Wizard and one of the more powerful, being descended from both Witch and Wizard stock. He added many new Spells—one of his longest-lasting was a popular **Unseen** (once used by Nicko Heap). Dan died at the young age of thirty-six.

LONGEST-SERVING: MYRIAM D. DROMENDURRY

Myriam was ExtraOrdinary Wizard for so long that most people in the Castle at that time could remember no one else. She became ExtraOrdinary Wizard at the age of twenty-two and retired on her ninety-third birthday because, she said, she was becoming a little forgetful. Myriam had thirteen Apprentices who all loved her dearly, and one of them, Julius Pike, became the next ExtraOrdinary Wizard.

OLDEST-SERVING: BRYNNA JACKSON

Brynna Jackson was a mediocre ExtraOrdinary Wizard and knew it, but she wanted something to be remembered for and this was all she could manage. She hung on to office for years longer than she should have. No one can force an ExtraOrdinary Wizard to retire, but they can drop heavy hints. For years the Wizard Tower resounded with the clanging of hints being dropped, but Brynna was deaf to them all—until the day after her ninety-third birthday.

FATTEST: BIG BRIAN BOOM

Brian Boom ate seven meals a day because he thought seven was lucky. But it wasn't lucky for Brian. He got wedged halfway up the narrow stairs to the Pyramid Library, and for three days no one noticed he was gone. After that, Brian **Stopped** the Wizard Tower stairs and walked instead. He lost a lot of weight but was not popular with the other Wizards, who also had to walk.

SHORTEST-SERVING: TAM THISTLE

Tam Thistle was ExtraOrdinary Wizard for three hours twenty-three minutes and thirteen seconds. Unfortunately she got her new robes entangled in the spiral stairs and you don't want to know the rest. No, really you don't.

THINNEST: TIMOTHY PAU?

No one really knows—it is hard to tell under all those robes. But Timothy Pau was apparently known as Thin Tim. And that, indeed, is all that is known of Timothy Pau.

LEAST TALENTED: BERT THE BASHER

A case of mistaken identity. A few days before his induction as ExtraOrdinary Wizard, Hamilton How was mugged by a footpad known as Bert the Basher. Bert found the Letters of Induction in Hamilton's pocket and, realizing that he looked a lot like Hamilton, decided to assume his identity and see—as he put it—"what he could get out of those Wizard dummies."

Bert toughed it out for a few weeks until Hamilton How turned up. Then Bert fled, taking ten gold plates from the dining service and the duty Wizard's best boots.

MOST TALENTED: _____

The pamphlet would not dare to venture a comment, as we know that this will be read by the current ExtraOrdinary Wizard (see below).

MOST RECENT: MARCIA OVERSTRAND

Not bad, all things considered.

MARCIA OVERSTRAND EXTRAORDINARY WIZARD

MARCIA OVERSTRAND grew up as the only daughter of an ancient Wizard family from the Far Countries. The family arrived at the Castle when Marcia was five years old after some embarrassing difficulty with her father's job as a minor Wizard and adviser to an Eastern Snow Princess. The young Marcia received little encouragement to take the extra **Magyk** classes at school, as her parents wished to distance themselves from **Magyk**, but, being Marcia, she insisted and they—as usual—gave in.

Naturally Marcia excelled at school. She knew that she wanted to be ExtraOrdinary Wizard, but she kept quiet about it until one day as a teenager when she had a huge argument with her mother and told her that she was going to be ExtraOrdinary Wizard, *so there.*

After the argument, Marcia moved out of the family home—an attic in a tall house in Snake Slipway, two doors up from the Van Klampff house—and rented a small room in the Ramblings from where she enrolled as a Hopeful in the Open **Magyk** classes that were run at the Wizard Tower for those who hoped to become Apprentices.

Her chance came suddenly. Silas Heap gave up his Apprenticeship to Alther Mella, and Alther wanted to replace him immediately. Alther had given a few lectures to the Hopefuls and he had been impressed with Marcia. He invited her—along with three other Hopefuls—to spend a day at the top of the Tower. It was no contest: Marcia was by far the best for the job as his next Apprentice, and despite her rather brusque air, Alther found that he liked her very much. Marcia really *cared*—about **Magyk** and, more importantly, about people.

65

Marcia enjoyed her Apprenticeship with Alther. For seven years and a day she and Alther argued, laughed and learned together. Marcia had not long completed her Apprenticeship—and survived the dreaded **Draw** for the **Queste**—when she came with him to help him out at his Welcoming Ceremony for the newborn baby Princess.

That evening, a profoundly shocked Marcia found herself wearing the Akhu Amulet and the purple robes of the ExtraOrdinary Wizard. It was what she had always wanted—but never like that. The old Castle saying, "Beware of what you wish for, lest it come true," has haunted her ever since.

Now Marcia has her own Apprentice, Septimus Heap. Septimus is remarkably young to be an Apprentice, but Marcia chose him after ten years of living without one—and Marcia knows best.

⬚ ⬚ ⬚ ⬚ ⬚ ⬚

ALL THOSE WHO HAVE BOUGHT Silas Heap's *I-C-U in the Castle Scorebook* may wish to know how to spot Marcia Overstrand and gain the top 100 points.

DESCRIPTION: Tall with dark, curly hair. Piercing green eyes.

SHE WEARS: Around neck (although usually hidden), lapis lazuli and gold Akhu Amulet. Purple double-silk cloak (lined with indigo-blue fur in the winter). Long purple silk tunic with small amount of gold embroidery. Gold and platinum ExtraOrdinary Wizard belt. Pointed purple python shoes.

N.B. If you see someone wearing all of the above but without the shoes, it is *not* Madam Marcia Overstrand.

A Guide to
How to Behave When Visiting the Wizard Tower

BY MADAM MARCIA OVERSTRAND
ExtraOrdinary Wizard

We, the Wizards of the Wizard Tower, firmly believe in access to all, and tours are available on alternate Monday afternoons. However, we reserve the right to refuse entry to those considered unsuitable. *Visiting the Wizard Tower is a privilege.* The following rules must be read before you enter the Tower. Please sign the "I accept" clause at the bottom, otherwise entry will be denied.

～⊛ GENERAL BEHAVIOR ⊛～

Remember that this is home to many Wizards, so please behave as you would in your own home (or at least as you would like people to think you behave). No screaming, shouting or swearing. No running, singing, dancing, playing ball games or skipping. No chewing gum, no musical instruments, no looking in the cupboards and no imported fruits or vegetables.

⤜ PETS ⤛

No pets allowed. Any smuggled hamsters will be speedily removed.

⤜ THE PASSWORD ⤛

The double silver doors at the main entrance are protected by the password. This will be whispered by your host Wizard and it is considered very rude to try to listen. In any case, you will not hear anything that is correct, as the password is self-scrambling. Please do not try shouting random words at the doors, hoping to get lucky. If you do, you will be asked to leave immediately.

⤜ THE MAGYK FLOOR ⤛

In the beautiful main vaulted entrance hall of the Wizard Tower you will notice that the floor feels somewhat like sand. *Do not* attempt to poke at it with your foot; it is a delicate, enchanted substance and difficult to repair. Stand still a moment and take time to watch for any messages. It will welcome respectful visitors if there are not more important messages to be relayed. Do not ask the floor to write something special for you—*the floor does not take requests.*

⤜ THE SPIRAL STAIRS ⤛

These are probably the most popular feature of the Wizard Tower with visitors—and the most commonly abused. These are moving spiral stairs and must be treated with caution. Children under ten are *not allowed* on the stairs.

- ✤ *Do not* attempt to mount the stairs unless accompanied by your Wizard guide.
- ✤ *Do not* attempt to instruct the stairs.
  Your Wizard guide will instruct them to turn.
- ✤ *Do not* run up the stairs while they are moving.
- ✤ *Do not* request stairs to be placed on emergency speed.
- ✤ Wizards have priority use, so please do not complain if one wishes to stop the stairs to get off or on.
- ✤ Obey the safety instructions of your Wizard guide at all times.

N.B. Rides are timed to ten minutes maximum.

∾ THE TWENTIETH FLOOR ∾

The top two floors of the Tower are home to the private rooms of the ExtraOrdinary Wizard. The spiral stairs stop at the twentieth-floor landing. Selected groups of visitors (those who have caused no trouble on the lower floors) may briefly get off the stairs and walk *quietly* along the landing to see the magnificent purple door that is the entrance to the rooms of the ExtraOrdinary Wizard. *Do not touch.*

∾ THE PYRAMID LIBRARY ∾

We regret that access to the Library is not available at present.

I hereby agree to accept the above terms and conditions and promise that I will abide by all instructions given by the Wizard guide.

Signed _____

The Journal of Marcia Overstrand

Entry #1

Something awful has happened. I know that I have always wanted to become ExtraOrdinary Wizard, but I never, never wanted it to be like this. But it is true. I am now the ExtraOrdinary Wizard, and my wonderful teacher and friend, Alther, is dead. Shot. And the dear Queen too and her baby girl as good as an orphan, for who knows where her father is?

Tonight I left the Princess out in the snow and waited until I knew that a certain someone (I dare not reveal who here, as even if I Seal this journal, it may still fall into the wrong hands) had taken her to safety. It is not the ideal home for a Princess, but it is the only home that I can think of.

Entry #3

Guards are everywhere. The Castle has been taken over. The Wizard Tower must stand firm. They will not dare touch us.

Entry #6

It is so sad, have just heard that the poor Heaps' seventh son died very soon after he was born. No one knows why. I do hope everything else is all right.

Entry #15
Morning

This place is a mess. I don't see why Alther couldn't have managed a few housekeeping Spells. Oh, how could I say that? Poor Alther. Anyway, today I have Removed the stains on the carpet. I put the stains on an old pair of socks and threw them down the rubbish chute—the rubbish chute is surprisingly useful.

Midnight

Very quiet up here tonight. All I can hear is the wind howling past the windows and—oh, what was that? I am getting jumpy. Oh, I _do_ miss Alther.

Entry #366

Alther finally **Appeared** while I was having breakfast. It was wonderful to see him again. The Supreme Custodian and his guards still search for the Princess, but they have no idea where she is. So far our plan is working.

But the Palace is ransacked, servants terrorized and drafted into the Custodian Guard. And Alther says the awful rumors of an army of children are _true._

Alther seemed tired and a little confused. Suggested he stay here for a few days. I shall be glad of his company. Talked into the night. Alther convinced that his old master, DomDaniel, is behind everything. Surely not?

On a lighter note, I told him about Alice Nettles's new job at the Port. Alther worried about whether he would be able to find her. He kept muttering, "A ghost may only tread once more where, Living, he has trod before." But I don't see what he is worried about—Alther went all _over_ the place. People used to moan to me about it all the time.

Entry #377

Alther made it to the Port and back! He found Alice in the Blue Anchor Tavern—which of course he could easily get into. Alice has just become Chief Customs Officer. Only trouble was

Alther got **Returned** from her official residence. Said being
Returned was horrible, felt like being sucked down the rubbish
chute, which I told him was plain silly. No one goes down rubbish
chutes. Couldn't believe that Alther had never been to the Chief
Customs Officer's official residence, but he said they gave very boring
parties and he couldn't be bothered. But Alice will figure it out.

Entry #687

Alther went to check on the Princess again today. He says she
is doing very well and is a lovely child. Doesn't look much like
her adoptive brothers though. Hmm, hadn't thought of that.

Entry #1,257

Alther has been going on about this Apprentice business. But
I don't _have_ to get an Apprentice. The truth is, I haven't seen
anyone with an ounce of talent—let alone anyone I could imagine
spending all that time with. Alther says people are starting to
talk, calling me fussy. Like I care.

Entry #3,001

Alther believes there is a spy in the Ramblings but can find
nothing out. Nothing. The trouble is, the Supreme Custodian has
begun holding his meetings in the Ladies' Washroom and Alther,
try as he might to get in, is always **Returned**—of course. Bother
and double bother.

Entry #3,650

Terrible news. An Assassin has been instructed. I _must_ speak
to Silas. I dread this day and what may come of it.

Entry #3,873

Woke late after another Dungeon Number One nightmare.

Have pounding headache. Must get up and check that
Septimus has brushed his teeth and combed his hair. He is
very disorganized at the moment. But after years in that awful
Young Army, who can blame him?

Entry #3,992

Another interesting day with Septimus. Who would have
thought that a son of Silas Heap's could be so quick to learn? We
moved on to **Hidden Seeks** today, and Septimus found them all.
Had yet another note from Sarah (apparently attached to a bag
of apples that was destroyed by the duty Wizard) asking him
to come to tea. Does she not realize that Septimus has important
work to do?

She sent me this letter:

> The Palace
> The Small Sitting Room
>
> Dear Marcia,
>   I hope you will, for once, allow Septimus to come
> to tea this Sunday. I can still count on the fingers
> of one hand the times I have seen him since we all
> returned from Zelda's. He is looking very pale. Is he
> eating properly? I am sending some apples for him.
>   Please tell him that his mother is so looking
> forward to seeing him.
>   Sarah Heap

Entry #3,993

I let Septimus go to tea with his parents against my better judgment, and what time did the child get back? Nearly midnight. These Heaps have no sense of responsibility.

Entry 4,438

Oh no no no no NO. I can't bear it. . . .

Dear Marcia,

I know that one day you will find this note because when I don't come back I know you will look everywhere in the Library and through all the Alchemie things that are there. I've never seen Marcellus's book in the Library, but I bet you know where it is. It is probably on that Sealed shelf. I hope you find it soon after I have gone so that you do not worry about me too much and so that you can tell everyone where I am. I am going to put it in the Almanac section of Marcellus's book. He is writing it for our Time — I mean your Time. It is not my Time anymore. I will put it in the day that I went so you will know where to look for it.

I want to say thank you, as I really liked being your Apprentice and I wish I still was, but I am Apprenticed to Marcellus Pye now. You must not worry, as it is not so bad, but I miss you all and if you can by any chance come get me (but I don't know how you can), I would be SO happy.

I have to go now. Marcellus is coming.

I came here through a Glass. Jenna will tell you.

Love, Septimus xxx

Entry 4,449

That dragon is a total health hazard and a disgrace. Have just *ReNewed* yet another window broken by all the disgusting stuff it coughs up. Why does it have to eat bricks? Those windows are not easy to *ReNew* anymore, after all this time. Had a delegation of Wizards yesterday complaining that the wretched beast traps them in the piles of poop and then tries to eat their cloaks. Enough is enough. To top it all off, got this pathetic note from old bossyboots down the road:

```
                              The Hermetic Chamber
                              The Manuscriptorium
                              13 Wizard Way


To: Marcia Overstrand, ExtraOrdinary Wizard
Re: Invoice number 44692


    The above invoice remains unpaid. To refresh
your memory, Marcia, this is for the damages
caused at the Manuscriptorium by your dragon.
You owe for three broken windows, a desk, four
chairs, six lamps and the cleaning bill from the
specialty cleaners we had to call in.
    Your payment is three months overdue, but I
trust I can expect it directly.
Sincerely,

(Miss) Jillie Djinn
CHS MTHAB MSSLA BSDC BSAA DFC*
(Diploma of Fish Counting: Distinction)
```

ALTHER MELLA

ALTHER MELLA was the ExtraOrdinary Wizard during a long period of peace in the Castle. Everyone liked Alther—and respected him too. He enjoyed the company of all kinds of people in the Castle and the Port and was also known to be a powerful Wizard. He had many Apprentices, the last two being Silas Heap and Marcia Overstrand. People were surprised when Alther took on Marcia. None of his previous Apprentices had been known as great students of **Magyk**—but Marcia was different. Some people even went as far as to say that Alther Mella had grown up at last.

A small shadow on Alther's reputation was the way in which he became ExtraOrdinary Wizard. Most of the inhabitants of the Castle had gathered in the Wizard Tower courtyard to watch the fight between the highly unpopular ExtraOrdinary Wizard DomDaniel and his much-loved Apprentice, Alther Mella. The fight took place on the golden Pyramid at the very top of the Wizard Tower, and it appeared that Alther pushed DomDaniel to his death. But things are not always as they seem.

It is worth noting here that Alther's protests that he did *not* push DomDaniel—that DomDaniel actually jumped—must indeed be true. Alther became ExtraOrdinary Wizard by a rare process of **Transformation**. ExtraOrdinary Wizards are created by a direct transfer of the Akhu Amulet from the previous incumbent—as happened with Marcia. This can also be taken by force, as DomDaniel did for his second—mercifully brief—period of office, and as, indeed, Alther did from DomDaniel. But Alther was also totally **Transformed**. During his horror-struck run down through the Wizard Tower, Alther's green Apprentice robes were **Transformed** to the purple robes of an ExtraOrdinary Wizard, and his very battered silver Apprentice belt **Transmuted** into the gold and platinum of the ExtraOrdinary Wizard. This is a rare occurrence and happens only at times of great importance. Incidentally, Marcia's belt was actually **Transmuted**, but she had to get her own robes from the Wardrobe Wizard on the tenth floor.

Now Alther wears only ghostly ExtraOrdinary robes, complete with the bloodstain on his chest where he was shot. He has long white hair, which is neatly tied back into a ponytail, and a well-trimmed white beard. This is because Alther had dressed up for his visit to the Queen and so is preserved forever in a way quite untypical of his usual everyday appearance.

Alther does not particularly like being a ghost. Who does? But, as he tells Marcia, it is better than the alternative. The one thing that Alther does enjoy about his ghostly state is his ability to fly. He loves the fact that he has lost his crippling fear of heights and is free to soar like a bird. His favorite occupation is skimming low along the river on a still night at full moon. At times like that Alther feels everything is right with the world.

Recently Alther has not done much flying. He has been taking care of Alice Nettles in her own Resting Time—the year and a day after entry into ghosthood. They have taken up residence in the Pavilion that Princess Jenna set up for them on the Palace Landing Stage, but Alther is looking forward to the time when he can take Alice by the hand and fly along the river with her by moonlight.

Alther Mella's Guide to Being Dead
TEN HANDY RULES FOR NEW GHOSTS

GHOSTWRITTEN BY SILAS HEAP

OKAY, SO THE WORST HAS ACTUALLY HAPPENED. You are dead. It's a big shock. In fact, some of you may not even realize you are dead. But you *are*. You have—as we so foolishly used to say—fallen off your perch, kicked the bucket and gone to a better place. Don't worry if you feel weird—it happens to us all eventually. It's a tough time, but you are not alone. With the help of my former Apprentice Silas Heap, I have put together this little pamphlet for all you new ghosts. We try and deliver it when and where needed and hope it may be of some use.

RULE ONE: Resting Time

This lasts for a year and a day. You will find that you are confined to the very spot where you died. This can be the most difficult time of all for some, as this very place may have bad memories for you. However, try to see it as a way of understanding what has happened to you. Do not use your time here as a way of getting back at those who are still Living in that place, however much you may feel they deserve it. As a ghost you should be above all that. For much of your **Resting Time**, particularly in the early days, you may be confused about where you are and why you are there. But, as the year and a day progresses, things will become clearer, and by the end of your **Resting Time** you will feel quite transformed.

RULE TWO: Move On

After your **Resting Time** you are free to leave the place where you entered ghosthood. Be brave and take that first step. Some ghosts never do, and this is a mistake. It can lead to a miserable and haunted time for all.

RULE THREE: Tread Once More

Be aware of this cardinal rule of ghosthood:

> A ghost may only tread once more
> Where, Living, he has trod before.

Most ghosts do not worry about this; they are happy to stick to familiar places. However, it does mean that you cannot use your ghosthood as an opportunity to go to all those wonderful lands you meant to visit when you were Living. My advice is to do the things you want to do *before* you die.

But I can pass on a useful tip—for all you sailors out there, you can still travel in your boat. Of course you cannot disembark, but you can see the world. Make sure someone keeps your boat in good order. If she sinks, you will be **Returned**. This also applies to horses (obviously not the sinking part), but unfortunately horses do not last forever. I have heard of some ghosts who have been **ReUnited** with the ghosts of their horses, but this is a complicated process. See our supplementary pamphlet *Advanced Ghosthood* displayed in the window of the Manuscriptorium and in the Hole in the Wall Tavern.

RULE FOUR: Returned

If you step outside your "trod before" zone, you will be **Returned** to the nearest place where you have trod before. Being **Returned** is a foul experience; the best way I can describe it is like being sucked into a screaming whirlwind. Unless you are very cautious, you will probably experience it once or twice.

RULE FIVE: Pass Through

This is an experience you will be bound to have. Being **Passed Through** is not as bad as being **Returned**, but it is no fun. This happens when a Living person—or a part of a Living person—**Passes Through** you. It may just be the wave of a hand or a complete body **Passing Through.** Either way it is not pleasant and makes you feel quite hollow for some minutes afterward. Best avoided by carefully watching where you are going. You cannot blame the Living for doing this, although some do seem to be particularly careless. But remember they cannot see you unless you **Appear** to them. See Rule Six.

RULE SIX: Appearing

Your first **Appearance** to the Living as a ghost is a big moment. Many choose never to **Appear** at all, and for all of us it is an important decision.

Some questions you may wish to ask yourself before you **Appear:**

- Who do I wish to **Appear** to?
- Is he or she expecting me?
- Is he or she in a situation where it is safe/not embarrassing for me to **Appear**?

Generally it is best to conduct your **Appearance** in the same way you would have conducted a visit when Living—make sure you will be welcome and do not stay too long. Remember, the Living may be upset at seeing you, particularly if you were close to them.

You yourself may also find the experience unsettling. Many

ghosts say that it was at their first **Appearance** that they truly realized that they were indeed a ghost—especially if they saw themselves in a looking glass.

Think carefully before you **Appear**.

RULE SEVEN: Flight

One of the perks of being a ghost. Enjoy it. The air above where you once trod is available to you at any height. I recommend low-level flying.

RULE EIGHT: Causing

Under some circumstances you may be able to **Cause** something in the Living world to move. This is not easy. Instructions can be found in our Advanced pamphlet. **Causing** is mentioned here for your information only.

RULE NINE: EATING

You can't. It's a shame, but you get used to it.

RULE TEN: GHOST ETIQUETTE

Be polite to all ghosts.

Be patient to older ghosts, known as Ancients. They can be very faint and confused—remember, you will be an Ancient one day.

Do not scare the Living for the fun of it.

Do not **Pass Through** other ghosts.

Top Tips for a Happy Ghosthood:

✝ Be sociable: visit the Hole in the Wall Tavern.

✝ Remember you are responsible for the atmosphere wherever you are—be positive.

✝ And no, things were *not* always better in the Good Old Days.

Once you are familiar with these rules, you may wish to read our new pamphlet, *Advanced Rules of Ghosthood*, on display in the window of the Manuscriptorium and inside the Hole in the Wall Tavern. Subjects include:

✝ New Forms: How, why and when

✝ Reuniting with those who die later: Pitfalls and pleasures

✝ Reuniting with those who died earlier: Pleasures and pitfalls

✝ Pets: Can a hamster be a successful ghost?

✝ Discomposing: How to get through walls the easy way

✝ Ghosts to avoid

✝ Haunting for pleasure

✝ On being **Gathered** (recommended reading for ex-ExtraOrdinary Wizards)

And much, much more!

SEPTIMUS HEAP

EPTIMUS HEAP spent the first ten years of his life as a boy with no name. All he had was a number: 412. Known as Boy 412, Septimus was one of the Expendables in the Supreme Custodian's Young Army. Septimus stayed alive by following orders and keeping quiet, and he survived the dangerous night exercises in the Forest because—unknown to him—many of the trees were looking out for him at the request of his shape-shifter grandfather, Benjamin Heap.

The day that Septimus nearly froze to death in front of the Wizard Tower was the day that changed his life. It threw his lot in with the Heaps and with Marcia Overstrand and began his voyage of discovery. He learned many things in those next few months: that people could be kind, that Wizards were not so bad, that cabbage sandwiches tasted good and that even Princesses were quite nice really. He also learned to his surprise that he was good at **Magyk**—the very **Magyk** that the Young Army had taught him to despise. Not only was he good at it, he was *so* good that the ExtraOrdinary Wizard actually wanted him to become her Apprentice—which was, he thought, just ridiculous.

But during his few months in the Marram Marshes with Aunt Zelda, Jenna and Nicko, Septimus changed. He shrugged off the shackles of the Young Army, he began to understand and trust people, and by the end of his time there, he decided that if Marcia Overstrand really did want him as her Apprentice then he would accept. And when he finally discovered who he was—Septimus Heap, the seventh son of Silas and Sarah Heap—Septimus felt his life opening out before him.

With the routing out of DomDaniel and all his cronies, and

the return of peace to the Castle, Septimus settled down to become Apprentice to Marcia Overstrand, and to try to get to know his family. This was at times a difficult balancing act—but something that he had never even dreamed would happen during his nightmare years as Boy 412.

So, if you were walking along Wizard Way on your way to buy a sausage sandwich from Wizard Sandwiches, how would you recognize Septimus? Like all the Heaps, Septimus has curly, straw-colored hair and bright green eyes. He does comb his hair, although Marcia does not always believe him when he insists that he has—*really*. You would notice the green Apprentice robes right away, as green is not a popular color in the Castle (most people go for more subdued hues). He would probably be wearing his green Apprentice cloak and he would definitely have on his silver Apprentice belt complete with all its little compartments for **Charms** and other bits and pieces. When you got close enough to say, "Hello, Sep!" (or just smile if you felt shy) you would see a beautiful gold Dragon Ring with its emerald eye on his finger. Septimus would return your smile or say hello; he is known around the Castle as a friendly, approachable Apprentice who has not gotten "above himself" as they say there. It is also easy to make him laugh.

A word of advice: if you see Septimus rushing along with Marcia Overstrand, it is advisable to do no more than give a brief wave. Marcia does not approve of distractions when Septimus is working.

EXTRACTS FROM
SEPTIMUS HEAP'S APPRENTICE DIARY

I saved this from the night 409 was lost overboard:

NOTIFICATION TO CADET OFFICERS 2 AND 11.

Night exercise for Boys numbers 405 to 415.
Cadet Officers 2 and 11 will:

- Assemble Boys at midnight.
- Silent-march Boys to waiting vessel
  at Slipway 5.
- Embark under battle silence.
- Advance vessel to Forest Landing
  Area 10.
- Disembark under battle silence.
- Complete night exercise 004a with
  double wolverine pit variation.
- At dawn embark surviving Boys.
- Return to Slipway 6.
- All Boys to return directly to duty.

* * * * * SPECIAL ORDERS * * * * *
It has come to the notice of the Cadet
Commander-in-Chief that some Cadet Officers
have been assisting the Boys when in danger.
This will NOT be tolerated. The Young Army
is a Strong Army. ALL Boys are Expendable.
Boys must sink or swim.

* * * * * * THE YOUNG ARMY * * * * * *

Rules and Regulations Applicable to:
Boy Expendables ranks I, II and IIIa.
(for IIIb see Y.A.R.R. appendix 5c)

Kit Regulations:
- Uniform must be clean and pressed AT ALL TIMES
- Boots must be polished AT ALL TIMES
- Daggers must be sharp AT ALL TIMES
- Backpacks must be in battle-ready order and
  ready for inspection AT ALL TIMES

Any Boy in breach of above regulations will
be allocated to the wolverine pit on the next
Night Exercise. NO EXCEPTIONS WILL BE MADE.

All Boys will be issued with:
- Tunic. Gray. 2
- Leggings. Gray. Pairs: 2.
- Y.A. Standard-issue Belt. Leather. 1.
- Dagger. Short. 1.
- Cloak. Gray. 1.
- Socks. Gray. Pairs: 2.
- Boots. Pair of. 1.
- Backpack. 1. (For contents of backpack see
  Quartermaster's regulations EB-B IVa.)

Chief Cadet Grade 1 Boys will also be issued
with:
- YA regulation hat with peak. Gray. 1.
- Rabbit Fur Jerkin. 1.
- Superior Boots. Pair of. 1.
- Socks. Superior-grade Wool. Gray. Pairs: 2.
- Dagger. Long. 1.

Any rank insignia will be issued on the first
of the month at the Commander's Parade and
will be sewn on IMMEDIATELY. Failure to do so
will result in withdrawal of ALL privileges and
allocation to the wolverine pit on the next
Night Exercise.

STANDARD ARMY TESTS (SATS)
MidWinter Feast Day Program

Rank: Boy (Expendable)   Number: 412   Age: 6

0400 hours
  Pack Junior backpack according to Young Army
  Regulations.
0423 hours
  Proceed to canteen. Regulation porridge to be
  eaten under battle silence.
0430 hours
  Commence ten-mile march under battle silence.
1000 hours
  Return to barracks.
1100 hours
  All Key Stage One rhymes to be recited. Boys
  shall recite until word perfect.

RHYME 1.
  Tomorrow's Future Today: Young Army is the
  Way. Hooray!

RHYME 2.
  On the Brink, Stop and Think.

RHYME 3.
  Who in the Castle is Number One?
  The Supreme Cust-oh-de-UN!

RHYME 4.
  Friends are enemies; enemies, friends,
  We don't need to make amends.

RHYME 5: Re: ExtraOrdinary Wizard. All Boys on
Wizard Tower guard must recite this ten times
before going on duty.
  Crazy as a cuttlefish, nasty as a RAT,
  Put her in a pie dish, give her to the CAT!

LEARN THE SEVEN BASYK TYPES OF SPELLS

TUTOR NOTES

Septimus, please note you will only practice the first four types of Spells until your sixth year. All Spells come in different levels of difficulty and <u>risk</u>. During your first year you will only do <u>level one</u>. I know you have tried at least two level threes (don't think I don't notice what you are doing in your bedroom), <u>but this must not continue</u>. Also note that these are simple categories and all Spells can be combined to produce compound Spells at an advanced level.

Read and learn pages 2 to 4 in Dan Forrest's BASYK MAGYK *Primer*, then list below the seven types of Spells with a brief description:

1. *Servant Spells:* e.g., to Find something that is lost

2. *Creature Spells:* to cause a creature to change

3. *Matter Spells:* to change matter

4. *Personal Spells:* to cause yourself to change

5. *Extra-personal Spells:* to cause another person to change

6. *Perception Spells:* to change how things are seen

 e.g., *Projections*

7. *Other Spells:* calling on the assistance of *Darkenesse*

TUTOR'S GRADE & COMMENT

A+ Very well done. Well remembered.

CREATURE SPELL
LEVEL ONE:
HOUSE MOUSE

TUTOR NOTES

Use a mouse from the kitchen. There is no need to go all around the Tower making a nuisance of yourself and certainly no need *whatsoever* to go traveling up and down the stairs all day looking for one. We will prepare the CHEESE CHARM this afternoon.

Instructions: First catch your mouse (see above). Hold securely in both hands and give the mouse the CHEESE CHARM to eat. Look the mouse directly in the eye and chant the INCANTATION in a low voice so as not to alarm the creature:

MOUSE OF MINE, LOOK AT ME,
MOUSE OF MINE, YOU WILL BE,
MOUSE OF MINE FOR A YEAR AND A DAY,
MOUSE OF MINE, YOU WILL NOT STRAY.

When the mouse finishes eating the CHEESE CHARM, you will have your House Mouse. Now answer the following questions:

1. How do you treat your House Mouse? *With respect.*

2. Where will you keep your House Mouse? *I may keep it in my pocket all day, but at night it must be free to come and go as it pleases.*

3. What will you feed your House Mouse? *I will feed it healthy food suitable for a mouse, and I will not give it sweets or chocolate.*

4. Name five functions of a House Mouse. *To be a companion, for running errands, to take messages to friends, to play board games and to fetch and carry small objects.*

CREATURE SPELL LEVEL ONE: HOUSE MOUSE

TUTOR'S GRADE & COMMENT

A- Well done. Your House Mouse is a little on the frisky side, and you had some trouble getting it to eat all of the CHEESE CHARM, but you persevered well. Apart from that, it was very good. Do you *really* want to call it Boris?

CHARMS:
BASYK THEORY
AND PRACTICE

TUTOR NOTES

We will spend this week in the Pyramid Library and on a field trip to the Manuscriptorium. You will also have an afternoon free to browse in the smaller bookshops along Wizard Way to see what CHARMS you can find.

Questions to be answered by the end of the week and handed in on Friday 5:00 P.M. latest:

1. Where can you find CHARMS? *Almost anywhere because people lose them. But usually in Magyk books tucked in a folded corner of the page.*

2. What is a CHARM? *A Charm is a small object that contains the Magyk imprint of the Spell and has the Spell written on it.*

3. Give seven examples of materials used to make CHARMS. *Cheese, parchment, diamonds, stone, haddock, silver, toast.*

4. Do you always need the CHARM to successfully complete a Spell? *No, but you will need it for the first time.*

5. What is the most popular CHARM in the Castle? *A parchment pink heart true-love Charm—yuck.*

6. How many CHARMS are in the Pyramid Library? *More than a million.*

7. Have you written a thank-you note to the Manuscriptorium for allowing you to see their rare and UNSTABLE CHARM collection? *Yes. I gave it to the boy at the desk. He is really nice.*

CHARMS:
BASYK THEORY
AND PRACTICE

TUTOR'S GRADE & COMMENT

~~B~~ *A* Haddock is <u>not</u> used for CHARMS. Were you trying to be funny? CHARMS are a serious business, Septimus. Also, "yuck" is not a suitable comment to be made in your homework. Apart from that you did well. And I am impressed with the CHARM you tracked down in Bertie's Book Heaven. I have never seen such an ancient and perfect scarab SAFECHARM before. Well done. In fact, on consideration, this is worth an A.

✠ PAPERS FROM ✠

THE PALACE

THE Palace

HOW TO GET THERE: From the river, land at the Palace Landing Stage. From the Castle, head south down Wizard Way; you can't miss the huge Palace Gate at the end of the Way.

WHO LIVES THERE: The Princess and her parents, Silas and Sarah Heap. Maxie the wolfhound and Ethel the duck. Merrin Meredith (unofficially). Numerous Palace ghosts.

WHAT YOU'LL FIND THERE: The ancient seat of the Castle Queens.

WHY YOU'D GO THERE: To visit the Princess or the Heaps, or to sneakily find a little attic room to live in.

WHY YOU WOULDN'T: The Palace is haunted and can be spooky. Some people find Silas Heap a little annoying.

So You Want to Visit the Palace

(OR WELCOME TO MY HOME)

A PAMPHLET BY SILAS HEAP

THE PALACE has not always been a place that just anyone can visit, but times have changed. My wife, Sarah, and I now welcome all on our guided tours.

The Palace Gate is open from 6:00 A.M. to 12:00 midnight. Please remember that we have a very Ancient ghost, Gudrun the Gate—oops, sorry, Gudrun the *Great*—on gate duty. It is polite to ask her permission to enter, but she will always give it. Once through the Gate, stop for a moment to admire this beautiful building. We believe the Palace to be one of the most ancient buildings in the Castle. It is constructed from the mellow yellow stone used in the olden times. The long, low lines of the building, with its ancient crenellations and turrets at each end, are like nothing else you will see in the Castle.

Proceed up the drive, past the well-tended lawns (courtesy of Billy Pot and his new mowing machine), and approach the wide plank bridge that crosses the ornamental Moat. Please *do not* dabble your fingers in the water. We have been trying to get rid of the infestation of snapping turtles, which were introduced by the Supreme Custodian in the Bad Old Days. We thought we had been successful but, after an unfortunate incident with an umbrella, it seems not.

Walk across the bridge and please announce yourself to the attendant on duty at the door. All tours meet up in the entrance hall and *must* wait for their tour guide to collect them.

Your tour will start at the Long Walk. This is one of the wonders of the Palace—a mile-long corridor that traverses the center of the Palace like a backbone. We've been told the Walk was once filled with paintings of past Queens, statues, treasures and trophies from all over the world. But since the Supreme Custodian sold the Palace's treasures to pay for his extravagant banquets, nothing has been the same. A Mr. Milo Banda—previous consort to our dear departed Queen Cerys—has sought to replace these treasures during his extensive trips to the Far Countries, but in my opinion the quality of the objects that can now be found scattered along the Long Walk is vastly inferior. The man has no taste.

Please note that on your tour we will not be visiting the Throne Room. My daughter, the Princess Jenna, has decided that she wishes the room to remain locked until the day she herself becomes Queen. This is out of respect to the memory of her mother, who was murdered in that very room, with the Princess Jenna herself only by chance escaping with her life.

You may notice that most of the rooms are at present unoccupied. While in the past the Palace was a busy place full of servants, we are no longer in the fortunate position of being able to continue this due to the raiding of the royal coffers in the Bad Old Days. We do hope one day to be able to return the Palace to its previous glory, but this may take some time.

But the Palace is not totally empty. My wife, myself and the Princess Jenna all live here, not forgetting our four-legged friend, Maxie, and Ethel, our duck. We also have two resident staff members—the cook and the housekeeper—and our volunteer door attendants all have rooms at their disposal here.

We wish to extend a warm welcome to all and invite everyone to visit our beautiful Palace. Details and prices of tours are posted on the gates. The Palace is a place for *all* the people of the Castle. We hope you will stop by!

Silas Heap

N.B. If you wish to contribute to the Palace Restoration Fund, please use the box by the Palace Gate for your donation. No money is left overnight.

A MIDWINTER FEAST GREETING

Dear Friends,

How quickly the time flies! Last MidWinter Feast was a little fraught and we apologize for not being in touch.

I know you will all be thrilled to hear that our youngest son, Septimus, whom we thought dead, is alive! Silas is sending out a pamphlet telling you how this wonderful thing came to be, but you can all imagine how happy we are to have our little Septimus with us once more.

Unfortunately, just before we were reunited, our Septimus was taken on as ExtraOrdinary Apprentice, and so he now lives at the Wizard Tower with Madam Marcia Overstrand. We do not see as much of him as we would like, but it is wonderful to know he is there. He is a very talented boy and excels at **Magyk**.

You may have heard that our lovely daughter, Jenna, has turned out to be the Princess. We always knew she was special, but it is still amazing to think that the little bundle that Silas found in the snow the night the Queen was assassinated is the true Princess.

All our boys are doing well, although Simon is having a little rebellion at the moment. He recently kidnapped Jenna and tried to kill Septimus, but we feel it was all a misunderstanding; he is a good boy, really. If you see him, please ask him to write his mother.

Sam, Edd, Erik and Jo-Jo are in the Forest learning Forest skills and becoming independent young men. We are very proud of them and hope that they will take time out of their busy lives to visit soon.

Nicko now has an Apprenticeship with Jannit Maarten at the renowned Castle Boatyard. We are told that he is a gifted boatbuilder and excelling at his Apprenticeship.

Please note our new address. After twenty-five years in the Ramblings, the Heaps have picked up sticks and moved into the Palace. There are many empty rooms, so please come visit us.

We hope your year has been as exciting as ours has been! We trust that next years' Heap Update won't be nearly as full of adventure, but you never know. Since we left the Ramblings life has been full of surprises!

With all good MidWinter wishes,
Your friends,

Sarah &
Silas Heap

JENNA HEAP

UNTIL SHE WAS TEN YEARS OLD, Jenna Heap thought she was the daughter of Sarah and Silas Heap. She lived with her six older brothers in a crowded, chaotic and happy room in the Ramblings. Jenna slept in a cupboard with its very own window that looked out over the river, which she loved.

For ten years Jenna lived a happy and secure life with her adoptive family, never dreaming that on her tenth birthday everything would change. That was the day Marcia Overstrand, ExtraOrdinary Wizard, came knocking on the door and changed Jenna's life forever. That was the day Jenna discovered that she was not a Heap but the Princess—and that there was an Assassin out to kill her.

Suddenly, Jenna was on the run for her life. But the Heaps stayed with her, and with the help of Marcia Overstrand and the Dragon Boat, Jenna overcame all the **Darke** forces that were against her.

On her return to the Castle, Jenna moved into the Palace with Sarah and Silas Heap and began to get used to the idea that one day, when the Time was Right, she would be Queen—although she is not sure whether she really ever wants the Time to be Right.

Jenna has a tutor for what she calls "Princess Stuff" and she also goes to school in the mornings at Snake Slipway Middle School. Jenna's tutor encourages her to practice talking like a Queen. Jenna has put this to good use at the Manuscriptorium—and enjoyed the experience.

Jenna spends as much time as she can with her adoptive brother Septimus. Whether they are flying on Spit Fyre—Jenna is Navigator—or just wandering through the Palace talking, there is no one Jenna would rather be with.

Jenna's Palace Diary

Private.
Keep Out.
Princesses Only!

MONDAY

Today Mum and Dad and I moved into the Palace. It's <u>huge</u>, and it is stuffed full of ghosts! Everywhere I go, especially at night, ghosts **Appear** and introduce themselves to me. They all tell me how pleased they are to have a real Princess here once again—so I suppose I must be a real Princess.

There is a really lovely ghost called Sir Hereward and he is on guard just outside my bedroom door. I have the bedroom that all Crown Princesses (that is what I am!) have had. I am glad Sir Hereward is there, as it is a little bit creepy. But the room is very beautiful and I suppose I shall get used to it—especially as it used to be my mother's bedroom when she was young. I like to think of her here when she was the same age as I am.

TUESDAY

Bo came over today and we went exploring in the attic. I met a ghost of a governess; her name is Mary. She kept calling me Esmeralda and telling me to be careful, which was a little spooky. I am glad Bo was there, even though she didn't see the ghost. Mum and Dad are really happy. They still can't quite believe that Septimus has come back. Mum went to the Wizard Tower to try to see him, but he was busy today. She's going to try again tomorrow.

WEDNESDAY

Mum had an argument with the Cook today. The Cook is very bossy and won't let Mum into "her" kitchen. Mum misses cooking, but the Cook says it is her job to cook the food and Mum's job to eat it—and we <u>have</u> to eat in the huge Palace dining room. Yesterday Mum sat at one end of the table—which is at least thirty feet long—and Dad sat at the other end and they couldn't even hear what each other was saying. So then they started doing signs, which they thought was really funny. Personally I thought it was silly.

THURSDAY

Nicko spent all day at the boatyard and didn't come back until really late. Nik told me that Jannit has offered him an Apprenticeship and he is going to tell Mum tomorrow. It will mean he has to live at the yard and I don't think Mum will be very happy. And I will miss him; we spent so much time together at Aunt Zelda's.

FRIDAY

I saw Boy 412—oops, Septimus—today! It was his day off so, as I haven't gone back to school yet, I was allowed to go to the Wizard Tower and meet him. I had forgotten what a weird place the Wizard Tower is; it smells very peculiar. Septimus came to us for tea and Mum didn't stop smiling. She kept trying to ruffle his hair; he looked a bit embarrassed, but he let her do it. Nik was around for a while and then he went to the boatyard. I don't think he has told Mum about the Apprenticeship yet. Septimus and I walked back to the Wizard Tower, and Marcia came down to meet us. And guess what? She told me the password to the Tower! How amazing is that? But I am not allowed to tell _anyone else_ what it is, so I can't write it here.

SATURDAY

Nicko told Mum about the Apprenticeship and Mum is very upset. I went for a walk to the Wizard Tower; I said the password and it _worked_! Those huge silver doors swung open and they were _totally silent_. Septimus was allowed out for an hour, so we went down to the boatyard and saw Nik. It was fun.

SUNDAY

Tomorrow we will have been here a whole week! Mum has spent all day in the herb-garden-to-be and Dad has decided to be a writer. He says he is sick of being a Wizard. He says he has always wanted to write, but living with so many children in only one room meant he could never think straight. Now he has a _huge_ room all to himself and has put up a notice on the door that says, PAMPHLETEER IN PROGRESS. QUIET! Sometimes I think my parents are a bit odd.

I am going back to school tomorrow and getting a tutor soon too. Must go; Bo is coming to sleep over and we are going exploring at midnight, but it is a secret. I like living here!

NOTES FROM PRINCESS LESSONS

🌿 A Princess must always walk with her head up and her back straight.

🌿 A Princess must speak slowly and clearly and not shout.

🌿 A Princess must smile when smiled at and not frown.

🌿 A Princess must learn to judge character.

🌿 A Princess must be fair, just and impartial.

🌿 A Princess must trust her instincts.

🌿 A Princess must listen.

🌿 A Princess must attend her Princess lessons.

🌿 A Princess must not sneak out of the Palace in the middle of the night.

MY HORSE

Today I got a horse! I love her—she is called Domino and she is beautiful. Here's what she looks like:

She is pure white, apart from six black spots where the saddle goes. Her mane and her tail are white too and really long, so I am learning how to keep them brushed and braided. I have a horse instructor—Mrs. B—from the farm where Dad bought Domino (good old Dad!). Mrs. B is staying with us for a month and teaching me everything about how to look after Domino and how to ride properly too. We go for a ride every morning before school and people wave to us, which is fun.

THE QUEEN'S ROOM
TOP SECRET. DO NOT READ!

This is secret! The Queen's Room is in the turret in the east end of the Palace, but only the True Queen and her descendants can see the door that leads to it. I found it because I am the Princess. I was able to open it with the key Aunt Zelda gave me, but Sep couldn't see the door at all!

The door to the room is gold with all kinds of patterns in it. There is a big keyhole right in the middle and only my key can open the door, which comes down like a drawbridge. Sep says that when I go into the Queen's Room, it looks like I'm walking straight through a wall and disappearing.

The room is smaller than you would expect and is surprisingly cozy. There is a fire burning in the grate, and a comfortable armchair is in front of it. I thought the chair looked like a really good place to sit, but I didn't. It was strange—I felt as though someone was already sitting there. Someone nice.

But the best thing about the Queen's Room is the cupboard. It has UNSTABLE POTIONS AND PARTIKULAR POISONS written on it—just like Aunt Zelda's! If you go into it and close the door so that it clicks shut, then open the right drawer, it takes you straight to Aunt Zelda's own **UnStable** Potions and Partikular Poisons cupboard. How amazing is that? That is how the Castle Queens have traveled to visit the Dragon Boat, and that is why it is called the Queen's Way.

HOMEWORK NOTES FROM
OUR CASTLE STORY
Queens: the Good, the Bad, the Crazy and the Slightly Nervous

THE GOOD

Chapter Ten: THE FIRST QUEEN

- ❧ Name: Not known, but some people call her Queen Eleanor the Wise.
- ❧ Age when succeeded to Throne: She did not succeed to the Throne—she arrived one morning in the Royal Barge. According to legend she was twenty-one at the time.
- ❧ Length of reign: According to legend it was one hundred and one years long.
- ❧ Known for: Being the first and founding the Palace. Also for being very beautiful. And good.

Chapter Eleven: THE QUEEN AND THE DRAGON BOAT

- ❧ Name: Queen Miranda
- ❧ Age when succeeded to Throne: Twenty-two.
- ❧ Length of reign: Thirty-one years.
- ❧ Known for: Miranda asked Hotep-Ra to stay in the Castle and build the Wizard Tower. She was the first Queen to visit the Dragon Boat.

Chapter Twelve: A CASTLE WITHOUT ALE

- ☙ Name: Queen Daniella (The Dry)
- ☙ Age when succeeded to Throne: Twenty-three.
- ☙ Length of reign: Five years.
- ☙ Known for: Closing all the Taverns in the Castle.

THE BAD

Chapter Thirteen: ETHELDREDDA THE AWFUL

- ☙ Name: Queen Etheldredda
- ☙ Age when succeeded to Throne: Forty.
- ☙ Length of reign: Approx. fifteen years. Ended with a suspicious drowning, although there is a legend that she never actually died and is imprisoned in the attic.
- ☙ Known for: Murdering her two baby daughters and trying to murder her oldest daughter, Esmeralda.

THE CRAZY

Chapter Fourteen: THE NIGHTGOWN QUEEN

- ☙ Name: Queen Doreen
- ☙ Age when succeeded to Throne: Sixteen.
- ☙ Length of reign: Ten years.
- ☙ Known for: Running along Wizard Way in her nightgown. Keeping ferrets in the Throne Room. Making her advisers pass a skipping test every week.

Chapter Fifteen: WHICH WAY DID SHE GO?

- Name: Queen Datchet III
- Age when succeeded to Throne: Thirty-two.
- Length of reign: Two years.
- Known for: Moving the East Gate Lookout Tower to the western side of the Castle and Closing the Gate. It is thought she did this after being hit on the head by a rotten bedpost, which caused her to lose all sense of direction. One morning she took the dawn boat to the Port and was never seen again. Queen Datchet III had no daughter and was succeeded by her younger sister, Queen Daphne II (Daphne the Dull).

THE SLIGHTLY NERVOUS

Chapter Sixteen: THE LESS AWFUL DAUGHTER

- Name: Queen Esmeralda
- Age when succeeded to Throne: Eleven, but her brother was Regent until she was well enough to start ruling when she was twenty.
- Length of reign: Thirteen years.
- Known for: Having bad headaches and wearing a very large crown. N.B. Are these two facts related?

SUNDAY

Said good-bye to Milo—I mean my father. I still can't get used to thinking of him as my father. Felt really annoyed with him. He just shows up with a lot of stuff for the Palace and then he goes straight off again on another trip. This time he brought a pair of gold dragons, which Dad says look cheap. He gave me a compass and said maybe one day I would go on one of his voyages with him and then it would be useful. But I am <u>never</u> going in one of his ships. Why should I? Felt really angry after he left and threw it across the room. Took Domino out, but it rained.

MONDAY

Mum is really worried about this Sickenesse that is sweeping through the Castle. No one—not even Marcia—can find a cure. Last week they opened up the Infirmary just outside the Castle in case the Sickenesse is contagious, and Mum is going over there a lot. Dad is thumping around in the attic.

TUESDAY

Mum spent the night at the Infirmary and did not come home until this morning. Mum is tired and grumpy. Even Sep is being a bit weird at the moment. He told me he's been reading about some old Alchemist and he thinks he knew how to cure the Sickenesse. But what use is it anyway—the Alchemist was alive <u>centuries</u> ago.

WEDNESDAY

Had an argument with Mum at supper. Mum said she does not want me leaving the Palace in case I catch the Sickenesse. Said I <u>have</u> to visit the Dragon Boat every day. Mum said I didn't. Am going to read for a bit.

LATER

I can't sleep. It is one o'clock in the morning. It has been a foul evening. I was reading in my bedroom and I had a visit from a horrible ghost—<u>Queen Etheldredda the Awful</u>. I am not usually scared of ghosts, but I was scared of her.

Decided to sleep in Mum's sitting room as the thought of that ghost coming back gave me the creeps. Fell asleep on the sofa (after taking off all the junk) and was woken up by Sep! Suddenly he was in the room, soaking wet, white and spluttering like he was half-drowned. And even worse, that Awful Etheldredda was there, saying that she had saved him—I don't think so.

And then, when I went to get Sep a dry tunic, Etheldredda ambushed me outside the door. It was horrible. She said that if I didn't do what she asked she would **"Reverse** my **ReClaime,** Granddaughter, and your darling adoptive brother will drown at midnight tomorrow."

I don't know what to do. I want to ask Mum, but she is at the Infirmary. Sep has told me all about **ReClaimes**—when you save people at the very moment they are about to die from some kind of accident. I am pretty sure he said they can be **Reversed**.

I just don't know what to do. Can't sleep.

Things I Will Do in the Palace
When I Am Queen

BY JENNA HEAP

I WILL:

Have a candle burning at every window.

——✄——

Ask lots of people to live there.

——✄——

Open up the Throne Room and
make it feel nice again.

——✄——

Have a system of bells so that
everyone can call one another.

——✄——

Get more stuff in the Long Walk—
lots of tapestries would be good.

——✄——

Keep candles burning day and
night down the Long Walk.

——✄——

Have big parties in the Ballroom.

——✄——

Open the summer house.

——✄——

Never eat ducklings.

——✄——

Find my mother's ghost.

DELIVERED FROM THE WIZARD TOWER BY MESSENGER

Received at Palace 10:00 A.M.

From: Septimus Heap

Dear Jen,

   Thank you for cutting Spit Fyre's toenails — or claws, I suppose they are now. He likes it when you do that! Hope you have a nice day and the tutor does not do too much silly princess stuff today. I have a few hours off this afternoon and will call in on you-know-who. He might just remember something.

Love to Mum and Dad.

         Love, Septimus xxxx

Marcellus didn't remember ANYTHING. Sep says they went all the way to the top of the house and then Marcellus forgot why.

Some Palace Ghosts That I Have Seen

BY JENNA HEAP, PRINCESS

ALTHER MELLA

Alther is not really a Palace ghost, but he is my top ghost of all time so he has to come first. I have known Alther since I was tiny. He is like a ghost-grandfather to me.

SIR HEREWARD

My second favorite ghost after Alther. He guards my room. He has only one arm and tells the same joke over and over again, but he is lovely and would do anything to protect me.

GUDRUN THE GREAT

She is an Ancient—an ExtraOrdinary Wizard ghost who lives at the Palace Gate. I don't know why. I suppose she likes it there. She is from the Lands of the Long Nights and is really nice but very faded. In the sunshine you can't see her at all.

GODRIC

He used to guard the Palace door, but now he sleeps in the big armchair in the hall. Sometimes he snores.

FARA FIELD

An old housekeeper. Has ancient uniform with lots of ribbons and carries a small piglet under her arm. She wanders around the battlements on the roof, where she says she can see danger coming from "farafield." I don't know what her real name is so that is what I've called her.

YOUNG WAINWRIGHT

He is a boy groom. I often see him curled up asleep in the corner of the stable. Domino likes him, so he must be okay. Sometimes he tries to help me brush her, which is a bit weird.

THE UNKNOWN PRINCESS

I think she is a bit crazy. I only see her at the full moon when she paddles in the ornamental Moat, waving her arms like a jellyfish.

SIR BRETTICUS-PETTICUS

He was a knight and a Wizard too, which is unusual—plus he married a Queen. I can't think what she saw in him—he is very rude. He told me that I did not look like a real Princess. He was killed by an **Unstable** Spell of his own creation and now he roams the Long Walk with his feet on fire. At least he lights up the place a bit.

MARY

Was once governess to Princess Esmeralda's poor baby sisters. She is convinced that I am Esmeralda and is always telling me to be careful. I do feel sorry for her, but sometimes I just wish she would cheer up. If I see her coming I try and go another way.

Dear Jen,

Came by to see you, but you were out with Mrs. B on Domino. Hope you had a good ride. Tonight there is a special evening at the WT, as one of the really doddering old Wizards is retiring. Marcia said I could ask you. Well, actually, she said, "It would be appropriate for the Princess to be present tonight, Septimus. Please give her this Invitation." Except I have lost the Invitation. Oops. But please come tonight, Jen. A party of Wizards (me included!) will pick you up at the Palace at 7:00 P.M. Can you wear your best tunic with the gold stuff around the hem and clean your boots? You know what Marcia is like. And your best cloak.

Looking forward to seeing you!

Love, Septimus xxxx

P.S. Marcellus did not remember a thing. Spent the entire time looking for his glasses.

Marcellus and his stupid glasses! But I had a lovely evening in the Wiz Tower and Marcia was really nice.

People (and Dragons) at the Palace Who I Like

BY JENNA HEAP, PRINCESS

HILDEGARDE PIGEON

You would not believe it, but Hildegarde once worked for the Council of the Custodians! She was employed in the Accounts Department, which she says spent most of its time trying to curb the lavish spending of the Supreme Custodian. She was transferred to the Sales Force, which forced the sale of <u>all</u> the Palace treasures. Hildegarde loved the old pictures and furnishings she had to sell, but as she said to me, she had to balance the books. Later though, she felt really bad about what she had done and she applied to take part in the Second-Chance Scheme. She was accepted for training as a sub-Wizard, which is part-time, and volunteered for door duty at the Palace to try to make amends. She told me that she longed to be called to the Wizard Tower to train as an Ordinary Wizard, but she knew she had to be patient.

Now Hildegarde is at the Wizard Tower but not quite as she had hoped—she is in the Infirmary. I do hope she gets better soon.

BILLY POT

Billy Pot is grumpy, but he is sweet too. He told me that he once owned a pet shop that only sold reptiles. Billy loved lizards and snakes, and he specialized in breeding purple pythons. (The biggest python that Billy Pot ever bred now lives in the backyard of Terry Tarsal's shoe shop.)

When the Supreme Custodian bought a colony of snapping turtles from Billy, he ordered him to move into the Palace to look after them and Billy dared not refuse. Billy's niece, Sandra, took over the pet shop and started selling fancy hamsters and fluffy rabbits, which Billy thinks are silly.

Sandra bought Billy's pet shop, and Billy set up the lizard lodges down by the river. He built the Contraption and, with his lizards, embarked on his never-ending quest for the perfect lawn.

But now Billy cares for a lizard much bigger than those he used to breed—a dragon named Spit Fyre.

SPIT FYRE

Only just arrived! He is down on the big field by the river where Billy used to grow vegetables. They have finished building him a huge kennel. They thatched it at first, but Mum pointed out that thatch and dragons don't go well together so now it has fireproof tiles. Mum's friend Sally

told the builders where to get them. I think having Spit Fyre here is going to be really interesting.

DELIVERED BY HAND FROM THE WIZARD TOWER
BY B. CATCHPOLE
Received at the Palace 7:30 A.M.
From: Septimus Heap

Dear Jen,

Can you meet me at Marcellus's place today? Have just had a note from him! It is really good. I think he has remembered some things at last. He has some stuff of Nicko's to show us and he says there may be a way for him to come back!!!! See you there.

Love, Septimus xxxx

Yay! I can't wait until midday. We are going to get Nicko back—I know we are!

Wizard Way

HOW TO GET THERE: Wizard Way runs between the Palace and the Wizard Tower. As the saying goes in the Castle: "All roads lead to Wizard Way."

WHO LIVES THERE: Scribes, printers and papermakers and anyone who likes to be in the center of things.

WHAT YOU'LL FIND THERE: A beautiful wide avenue lined with trees and tall silver torch posts. The buildings are the oldest in the Castle, and they are home to everything to do with the written word. Here you will find the fabled Manuscriptorium.

WHY YOU'D GO THERE: If you need Spells, Charms, pamphlets or just a book to read. You might have an appointment at the Manuscriptorium. Or you might just want to buy a Wizard Sandwich, sit on one of the benches in the shade of the trees and see if you can spot the ExtraOrdinary Wizard's Apprentice wandering down to the Palace.

WHY YOU WOULDN'T: You might get asked to pick up litter by the Wizard Way Conservation Society Representative.

The Shops and Services of
Wizard Way

An Informative Guide by the
Wizard Way Conservation Society

{ A MESSAGE FROM THE WIZARD WAY CONSERVATION SOCIETY:
Take your litter home. }

Whether you are a day-tripper from the Port or a resident of the Castle, there is a myriad of surprises and delights to be found on Wizard Way.

To make your shopping experience a pleasant one—and to guide you to some of the more unusual establishments—the Wizard Way Conservation Society has produced this handy map with a brief description of some of the more interesting destinations. Please note that we cannot be held responsible for the goods and services offered in these establishments. *Caveat Emptor!**

*For translation we suggest you visit Larry's Dead Language Translation Services at number 67 number 1 on the map.

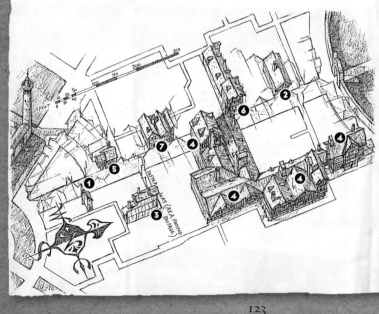

❶ Larry's Dead Language Translation Services

❷ Bott's Wizard Secondhand Cloak Shop

❸ Tarsal's Fine Boots and Shoes

❹ Wyvald's Witchy Bookshop

❺ Wizard Sandwiches

❻ The Magykal Manuscriptorium and Spell Checkers Incorporated

❼ Sandra's Palace of Pets

① Larry's Dead Language Translation Services: A small cubbyhole of a shop with room only for a desk, which is occupied by Larry himself. Will translate any dead language for a small fee.

PROPRIETOR: Larry

Larry can be a little irascible. When we asked him his surname for the purposes of this guide we were told, "Antiquis temporibus, nati tibi similes in rupibus ventosissimis exponebantur ad necem."*

In the Good Old Days, children like you were left to perish on windswept crags.

② Bott's Wizard Secondhand Cloak Shop: Formerly located in the Ramblings, Mr. Bott's popular shop now has an impressive frontage on Wizard Way. Note the ornamental green dragons and crouching purple lions. Mr. Bott tells us that he carries only the finest pre-loved fashions for the discerning Wizard—mainly cloaks. All garments are **Deep-Cleaned** and **Anti-Darke** treated. Also available: tunics, shoes and some Ordinary Wizard belts.

PROPRIETOR: Mr. Bott (the younger)

Mr. Bott took over the Secondhand Cloak Shop when his father retired thirteen years ago. He is inclined to be talkative but is very helpful.

TIP FOR SHOPPING AT BOTT'S:

Bring a magnifying glass—the labels on the cloaks are very small.

③ Tarsal's Fine Boots and Shoes: Follow Instep Way—a small dead end off Wizard Way—and you will find Terry's shop at the end.

PROPRIETOR: Terry Tarsal

Terry is a master craftsman and a gifted shoe designer. He will make shoes to your own specifications, repair a shoe while you wait and give advice on shoe care (whether you ask for it or not). Although famous for the purple python shoes he creates for ExtraOrdinary Wizard Marcia Overstrand, Terry Tarsal has asked the Wizard Way Conservation Society to point out that he will not make any further snakeskin designs.

SERVICES:

» Heel repair
» Toe repair
» New soles
» Stretching

» Restoration
» Dragon poop removal
  (*price on application*)
» Custom orders (*no snakeskin*)

Tarsal's Fine Boots and Shoes
Half-price Sale!

2 PAIRS red worker's clogs. Size: Extra large. New.

4 PAIRS green worker's clogs. Size: Extra large. New.

10 PAIRS pink hippo children's dance pumps. Assorted sizes. Used once. Very good condition.

1 PAIR red boots with blue laces. Child size: extra small. New.

1 PAIR pointy purple python shoes. Large size. Small (unnoticeable in the opinion of Mr. Tarsal) tear on heel.

❹ Wyvald's Witchy Bookshop: Wyvald's Witchy
Bookshop is the largest of the many bookshops on Wizard Way.
It is the premier carrier of all literature relating to the world of
witches and contains a vast uncataloged stock of old **Magy**k books.
The bookshop extends back for nearly a quarter of a mile and has
taken over at least four other houses behind it.

{ A MESSAGE FROM THE WIZARD WAY CONSERVATION SOCIETY:
*For your safety, we recommend that before visiting Wyvald's you tell
someone where you are going and at what time you expect to return.
We will only send our search-and-rescue party on that basis.* }

PROPRIETOR: Tom Wyvald
You may have seen Tom Wyvald striding along in his purple cloak
and long black tunic. The wearing of purple cloaks is discouraged
by the Wizard Tower, but Mr. Wyvald is, as he often points out, free
to wear whatever color he likes. You will discover that he finds it
amusing to be mistaken for the ExtraOrdinary Wizard.

Wyvald's Witchy Bookshop

THIS WEEK'S
RECOMMENDATIONS:

FROM THE ROMANTIC NOVEL BIN:
Meet Me at the Witching Hour
by Desdemona Dream

FROM THE WITCHERY WALL:
Harnessing Hexes
by Algaric and Pugh

FROM THE PAMPHLET PARADE:
Top Ten Counter-Feet Tricks
by Silas Heap

FROM ROYALTY ROW:
Our Princess: An Unauthorized Biography
by Pinkie Pry

FROM THE ARCANE AREA:
Theories of Time: A Book for Beginners
(author unknown)

FROM THE UNLUCKY DIP:
A Brief History of the Sheeplands
by Fred Partridge

❺ Wizard Sandwiches: *First Floor, Number 44 Wizard Way.* This facility is featured in *The Egg-on-Toast Restaurant Guide.* The Wizard Way Conservation Society wishes to point out that we have not given approval to the current door decoration of this establishment.

{ A MESSAGE FROM THE WIZARD WAY CONSERVATION SOCIETY:
Take your sandwich crusts home. }

❻ The Magykal **Manuscriptorium and Spell Checkers Incorporated:** *Number 13 Wizard Way.*
Recognizable by the chaotic stacks of papers in the windows. Door has recently been repainted in unauthorized color.

PROPRIETOR: Chief Hermetic Scribe, Jillie Djinn
    Miss Djinn is the latest in a long line of prestigious Chief Hermetic Scribes, the top position at the Manuscriptorium. She is a valued adviser to the Wizard Way Conservation Society on procedural matters and litter.

ADVICE FOR THE FIRST-TIME VISITOR TO THE MANUSCRIPTORIUM:

» Always go to the front desk first. Do not attempt to enter the Manuscriptorium itself.

» Be considerate! This is a place of work and study.

» The Chief Hermetic Scribe is available by appointment ONLY. Please make your appointment with the Front Desk Clerk and arrive ON TIME.

» Safety advice: do not approach the Wild Book Store at any time.

LIST OF SERVICES AVAILABLE TO THE PUBLIC:

» Old, UnStable Spells checked and ReStablized.

» Order copies of formulas, conjurations, incantations.

» Transcription of Spells, letters, manuscripts, poems, tomes, parchments, declarations, treaties and other texts.

» Calculations, Predictions and Astronomical Answers available if pre-booked.

» Some secondhand Spells for sale.

» Safe storage for Darke materials.

» Conservation, Preservation and Protection service available. See brochure for details.

» In conjunction with the Wizard Tower, the Manuscriptorium offers many arcane services. These are not advertised, and to find out more we suggest you book an appointment with Miss Jillie Djinn or with the duty Wizard at the Wizard Tower.

NOTICE

The Manuscriptorium wishes to announce that the annual Entrance Examination will take place on the thirteenth of this month at 7:13 A.M. Success in this—with rare exceptions—is a requirement for employment at the Manuscriptorium. Please collect an entry form from the Front Office and return by the eleventh of the month at 5:02 P.M.

Sandra's Palace of Pets: Once owned by Billy Pot. Now Billy's niece, Sandra, has taken over the business. Bunnies, kittens, hamsters—if it's fluffy, Sandra will stock it.

PROPRIETOR: Sandra Pot

Sandra has turned the previously basic (and smelly) lizard-breeding store into a pastel-painted palace for cuddly pets.

SERVICES:

- » Complete grooming service: perfumed shampooing, nail clipping, fur trimming, teeth whitening.
- » Hamster homes interior design service.
- » Complete personal shopper wardrobe service for tiny dogs.
- » Designer pet carriers—take your loved one everywhere you go!
- » Pet counseling and advice service for nervous pets or owners.
- » Ask about our breeding program (pets only).

{ A MESSAGE FROM THE WIZARD WAY CONSERVATION SOCIETY:
Take your pet's poop home. }

SANDRA'S PALACE OF PETS

Pets currently looking for the new person in their life:

BRIAN, BARNEY, BILLY, BRENDA, BARRY, BOFFY AND BEN
Baby mice, ten days old.

DAVE, DINAH, DIXIE AND DILBERT
Guinea pig family who wish to stay together.

PING-PONG
Exotic gerbil. Temperamental.

PRINCESS
Small chinchilla. Fussy about food.

Chief Hermetic Scribes, Past and Present

TERTIUS FUME

The very first Chief Hermetic Scribe, whose ghost still guards the Vaults. As boys, Tertius Fume and Hotep-Ra (the very first ExtraOrdinary Wizard) were the closest of friends. After Hotep-Ra fled his home country, Tertius Fume, who was at that time a loyal friend, set out to look for him. Many years later Tertius Fume arrived at the Castle and was joyfully greeted by Hotep-Ra. Tertius Fume was amazed by what he found. Not only was his friend in the process of finishing the incredible Wizard Tower, he was now loved and respected by all and was the closest of friends with the beautiful Queen. Tertius felt a little put out—he had come to rescue his grateful friend and now all he could do was bask in his friend's reflected glory.

But Hotep-Ra was his usual generous self. He set Tertius Fume up in a large house at 13 Wizard Way and, when Tertius expressed an interest in starting up what he called a Scribe House, Hotep-Ra gave him all the help possible. It was a terrible shock to Hotep-Ra when he returned to his beloved Dragon Boat from one of his visits with the Queen and discovered that Tertius Fume had declared a State of Emergency, installed himself as Locum ExtraOrdinary Wizard and taken over the Wizard Tower. Hotep-Ra was forced to oust his friend and banish him.

Tertius Fume made three of his scribes accompany him into banishment, one of whom, it is rumored, killed him.

WALDO WATKINS

A quiet man and a much-respected Chief Hermetic Scribe. For ten long years, Waldo bravely held out against the Supreme Custodian's demands for putting the Manuscriptorium to **Darke** uses. But his refusal eventually cost him dearly. Unlike many Chief Hermetic Scribes, Waldo chose to live outside the Manuscriptorium rather than in the apartment above it. Late one night, on the way back to his little house within the Castle wall, Waldo was ambushed by a troupe of Custodian Guards and was never seen again.

HUGH FOX

Hugh Fox had been an unremarkable scribe for twenty-five years when, to everyone's amazement, he was **Picked** to become Chief Hermetic Scribe. DomDaniel wanted a Chief Hermetic Scribe who would do his bidding and unlock the secrets of *The Undoing of the* **Darkenesse**—a book that he had snatched from Marcia Overstrand—and he fixed the **Pick**. Everyone knew he had done this, but no one was brave enough to say anything. But they all wondered who should have been Chief Hermetic Scribe instead.

JILLIE DJINN

It was Jillie Djinn who should have been **Picked** instead of Hugh Fox. This may surprise you—it surprised the author of this biography too. It is Marcia Overstrand's opinion that some people seem promising, but when they assume authority they change for the worse. She considers that Miss Djinn is one of these people. Madam Overstrand also considers that while Jillie Djinn is undoubtedly a good person, her lack of skills in assessing people's true characters may put the Manuscriptorium in some danger. Jillie Djinn is extremely knowledgeable—and awfully boring.

SOME EMPLOYEES OF THE MANUSCRIPTORIUM

O. BEETLE BEETLE

Beetle grew up in the Ramblings in two rooms beneath the Heaps, and Beetle's earliest memories are of his mother banging on the ceiling with a broomstick, yelling, "For heaven's sake, be *quiet*!"

Beetle was an only child and lived alone with his mother. Beetle's father, Brian Beetle, died before he was born after being bitten by a spider hidden in a box of bananas.*

At the age of eleven, much to his mother's delight, Beetle passed the highly competitive Manuscriptorium Entrance Examination and was taken on as General Dogsbody. When the Inspection Clerk fell off his sled, Beetle was entrusted to take over the weekly inspections of the Ice Tunnels. Beetle is Septimus Heap's best friend. They share a love of FizzFroot and a hatred of **Darke Magyk.**

---

*You may have read elsewhere that Beetle grew up with both his parents, but we regret to say that this is not true. Some of our sources are not always reliable. Also Beetle had a habit, when young, of pretending that his father was still alive and this has led to some confusion around the Castle.

COLIN PARTRIDGE

Colin had once been unwillingly recruited into the Custodian Guard. He was from a small village on the edge of the Sheeplands. Partridge was a dreamy child who spent his days minding his father's sheep—and losing more of them than his father cared to count. Colin's father despaired of his son. So when the Custodian Guard Recruiting Party arrived at the Partridge sheep farm promising to "make a man out of your son," Partridge's father had young Colin packed and ready in no time. Luckily for Colin, he arrived at the end of the Supreme Custodian's regime. He signed up for the Second-Chance Scheme and was snapped up by the Manuscriptorium. Partridge loves being a scribe and has no wish to return to losing sheep.

BILL FOX

Known to all as Foxy, he is the son of the disgraced ex–Chief Hermetic Scribe, Hugh Fox. Foxy, a lowly scribe, is extremely tall and thin and prone to fainting spells, but despite his being a bit of a wimp, Beetle likes Foxy. It is Foxy who introduced him to sausage sandwiches, and in an emergency in the Manuscriptorium, it is to Foxy whom Beetle will turn. Foxy does his best but often ends up in the Manuscriptorium infirmary in times of trouble. Jillie Djinn terrifies him, but Foxy enjoys his work.

ROMILLY BADGER

A new recruit who scored highly in the last Manuscriptorium Entrance Examination. Romilly has beautiful handwriting and a wicked sense of humor. Jillie Djinn has already had to speak to her about laughing on duty and bad timekeeping. Partridge very much hopes that she will not be dismissed.

EPHANIAH GREBE

The Manuscriptorium's Conservation, Preservation and Protection Scribe. He lives in the cellars under the Manuscriptorium and is rarely seen aboveground. Ephaniah had only just begun work at the Manuscriptorium when he was ambushed by a Rat Hex. It was a permanent Hex, but Morwenna the Witch Mother managed to undo some of the effects, leaving Ephaniah as part rat, part man. Ephaniah is a skilled and painstaking Conservation Scribe and can rescue even the most damaged papers, Spells and keepsakes.

How the Chief Hermetic Scribe Is *Picked*

✦✦ STEP 1 ✦✦
The current Chief Hermetic Scribe must die or retire.

✦✦ STEP 2 ✦✦
Each Manuscriptorium scribe places his or her pen into the large enameled **Draw Pot**.

✦✦ STEP 3 ✦✦
The outgoing Chief Hermetic Scribe, or the most senior scribe, takes the **Pot** into the Hermetic Chamber. It is left there overnight.

✦✦ STEP 4 ✦✦
In the morning, the youngest scribe is sent to the Chamber. One pen will be lying on the desk while all the others will remain in the **Pot**.

✦✦ STEP 5 ✦✦
Whoever is the owner of the pen on the desk is the new Chief Hermetic Scribe.

A Note: The **Draw** has been used for thousands of years. Only the best are **Picked**. Most scribes toil away their entire lives without ever being **Picked**. The position of Chief Hermetic Scribe is a great honor, and those **Picked** must be serious, dedicated and fair. And preferably not given to counting haddock.

DAILY APPOINTMENT DIARY OF
JILLIE DJINN, CHIEF HERMETIC SCRIBE (CHS)

DIARY KEEPER	O. Beetle Beetle

Monday

TIME: *9:22 A.M.*

WITH: *Silas Heap*

REASON FOR APPOINTMENT: *To ask for twenty-one pamphlet copies at discounted Ordinary Wizard rate.*

NOTES: *Three-and-a-half minutes late. CHS refused to see.*

ACTION: *OBB agreed to OW discount. Scribe employed: Scribe Foxy. To be collected 9:00 A.M. tomorrow.*

TIME: *2:55 P.M.*

WITH: *Terry Tarsal*

REASON FOR APPOINTMENT: *Delivery of shoes.*

NOTES: *On time.*

ACTION: *CHS declared shoes unsatisfactory. Rescheduled for Tuesday 10:08 A.M.*

Tuesday

TIME: *9:00 A.M.*

WITH: *Silas Heap*

REASON FOR APPOINTMENT: *To collect pamphlets.*

NOTES: *Arrived 10:07 A.M.*

ACTION: *OBB handed over pamphlets. Work satisfactory, apart from one pamphlet slightly smudged. Not charged for. Full payment received.*

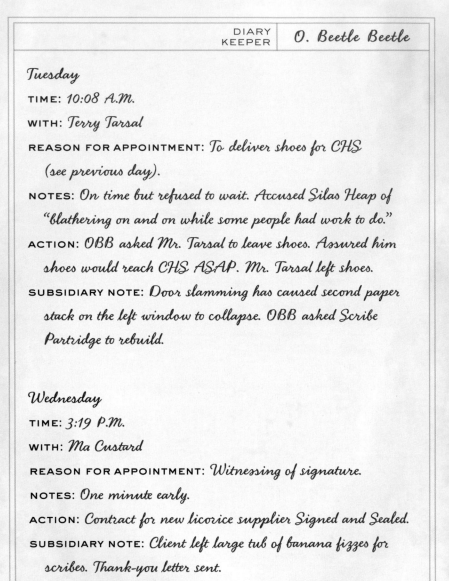

DIARY KEEPER	O. Beetle Beetle

Tuesday

TIME: *10:08 A.M.*

WITH: *Terry Tarsal*

REASON FOR APPOINTMENT: *To deliver shoes for CHS (see previous day).*

NOTES: *On time but refused to wait. Accused Silas Heap of "blathering on and on while some people had work to do."*

ACTION: *OBB asked Mr. Tarsal to leave shoes. Assured him shoes would reach CHS ASAP. Mr. Tarsal left shoes.*

SUBSIDIARY NOTE: *Door slamming has caused second paper stack on the left window to collapse. OBB asked Scribe Partridge to rebuild.*

Wednesday

TIME: *3:19 P.M.*

WITH: *Ma Custard*

REASON FOR APPOINTMENT: *Witnessing of signature.*

NOTES: *One minute early.*

ACTION: *Contract for new licorice supplier Signed and Sealed.*

SUBSIDIARY NOTE: *Client left large tub of banana fizzes for scribes. Thank-you letter sent.*

DIARY KEEPER	O. Beetle Beetle

Thursday

TIME: *10:12 A.M.*

WITH: *Marcia Overstrand*

REASON FOR APPOINTMENT: *Not given.*

NOTES: *Sixteen minutes late but insisted on being seen.*

ACTION: *New appointment.*

TIME: *10:28 A.M.*

NOTES: *On time.*

ACTION: *CHS provided Scribe Badger to facilitate access to Hidden shelf number three.*

TIME: *4:02 P.M.*

WITH: *Silas Heap*

REASON FOR APPOINTMENT: *Counter-Feet Sealed Box repair.*

NOTES: *Three-and-a-half minutes late.*

ACTION: *CHS refused to see. Box to go in night basket for EG.*

Friday

TIME: *2:16 P.M.*

WITH: *Marcia Overstrand*

REASON FOR APPOINTMENT: *Not given.*

NOTES: *Arrived 2:10 P.M. Requested to be seen immediately. Refused to wait until appointment time.*

SUBSIDIARY NOTE: *Scribe Partridge rebuilt second paper stack on the left window again.*

Beetle's
INSPECTION CLERK DAYBOOK
* *

O. BEETLE BEETLE'S VERY OWN
HISTORY OF THE ICE TUNNELS
(work in progress)

Dear readers,

You may wonder why no one has ever told you about the Ice Tunnels. Well, you are not alone. Even though I am the Ice Tunnel Inspection Clerk, no one has ever told <u>me</u> anything either. But here is some stuff I have worked out.

1. *The Ice Tunnels used to be just tunnels without ice.*

2. *In the old days, officials used the Tunnels to travel around the Castle underground.*

3. *Almost the entire Castle is connected by the Tunnels. Weird . . .*

4. *The Tunnels were sealed by the Emergency Freeze. This happened so fast that thirty-nine people were trapped*

MY SLED

ADD AERODYNAMIC
WINGS ONTO THE BACK.

ADD A POINTED NOSE
TO THE FRONT FOR
MORE SPEED.

SEP'S SLED

WIZARD TOWER SLED

THE ICE TUNNELS

ONCE-A-WEEK INSPECTION DUTIES:

Travel the Ice Tunnels on Manuscriptorium Sled.

Check that all the hatches remain **Sealed**.

Report any suspicious hatches, e.g., with clear ice indicating recent **ReSealing**.

ONCE-A-MONTH INSPECTION DUTIES:

Travel every tunnel, even those without hatches.

Test ice samples at specified areas.

Report to CHS.

SAFETY PRECAUTIONS:

Always secure sled, as it will wander off if left unattended.

Do not breathe in while Ice Wraith passing.

Always inform duty scribe of time expected to return.

Always **ReSeal** hatch to Manuscriptorium.

BEETLE'S ICE TUNNEL INFO

FAVORITE SPOT: *The high slope on the way to the Van Klampff Hatch. The perfect spot for the Reverse Whizz jump.*

LEAST FAVORITE SPOT: *The tunnel to the Palace kitchen hatch. Too thin for any tricks. Also feels creepy.*

GHOSTS: *Usual mix of officials, Wizards and tramps. Avoid those trapped in Emergency Freeze if you can. Some of them are still panicking. Not nice.*

ICE WRAITHS: *The worst is Moaning Hilda. Hold your breath as she goes past or she'll freeze the breath inside you. Cover your ears or she'll burst your eardrums. Other Ice Wraiths much less powerful.*

MOANING HILDA

BEST SLED MOVES

JUMP: *Free catching air at the top of a steep hill.*

DECK-UP: *Riding on the rear edges of the runner.*

BACKWARDS ALLEY: *Riding backward.*

SPIN REVERSE WHIZZ: *Once around and then coming to a stop with a backward slide.*

DOUBLE SPIN REVERSE WHIZZ: *Twice around and then coming to a stop with a backward slide.*

BACKWARDS ALLEY SPIN-AROUND WHIZZ: *Coming to a stop from the backward position, then with a spin at the end and a sliding stop. The best!!!*

JILLIE DJINN ALWAYS
SCOLDS ME WHEN I
SPEND TOO MUCH TIME
IN THE ICE TUNNELS.

MR. AND MRS. GRINGE OF THE NORTH GATE GATEHOUSE

GRINGE, THE GATEKEEPER

No one in the Castle knows Gringe's first name—or so he thinks. But the writer of these biographies has done her best to find out as much for her readers as possible. She can reveal here that the keeper of the North Gate gatehouse once answered to the name of Augustus—although he no longer does so, as the writer found out last week. In fact the writer strongly recommends that you do *not* use this form of address if you want to use the North Gate drawbridge.

Augustus Gringe is married to Theodora Gringe. They met in the Port and came to the Castle for a better life. At first they had a hard time and lived in a ramshackle shelter beneath the Castle wall. When Rupert was born, Gringe was determined to do better for his family. One day, when the Bridge Boy at the North Gate was injured by a loose chain, Gringe helped out. It was not long before his strength and reliability were noticed and he was asked to be stand-in Gatekeeper. Two years later, when the Gatekeeper retired, Gringe took over and at last his family had a proper roof over their heads.

The Gringes now have two children, Rupert and Lucy. Gringe is proud of what his son, Rupert, is doing and often talks about him, but he refuses to discuss his daughter, Lucy. Mrs. Gringe has been known to tell her closest friends that her husband has never gotten over Lucy running off with Simon Heap. He worries that Lucy will never forgive him for locking her up in the gatehouse after the Custodian Guards dragged her back from the Chapel, where she and Simon had secretly gone to get married.

Gringe is not a big fan of the Heap family. Gringe does not trust Wizards, he thinks that **Magyk** is "an easy way out of yer troubles" and he also had no end of problems with the high-spirited Heap boys playing Chicken on the drawbridge when they were little. When he asked Silas Heap to stop them, Silas just laughed and told him, "Boys will be boys." After Lucy attempted to elope with Simon Heap, Gringe's dislike of the Heaps increased.

But since Gringe realized that Silas did not approve of Simon either and saw how worried he and Sarah were about their children, he has felt some sympathy for the Heaps. The turning point came when Gringe found out that Silas had a **Magyk** set of Counter-Feet (Gringe's favorite game and his one exception to his dislike of **Magyk**). Gringe has now decided that Silas Heap is not so bad after all, although when asked by this biographer if they were friends, he refused to answer and went off to yell at the Bridge Boy.

THEODORA GRINGE

Known to all as Mrs. Gringe, Theodora has been the driving force behind the Gringe family's reversal in fortune. When the family was existing in their ramshackle shelter below the Castle wall, it was Theodora who told Gringe that the Bridge Boy had had a terrible accident and he must get down there *right now* and lend a hand. Gringe did not see why he should, but Mrs. Gringe did. And she was right.

Mrs. Gringe looks after the accounts at the gatehouse and makes sure the money is clean before it is put in the gatehouse coffers. Once a month she supervises its transport to the Castle Treasury, where Gringe's salary is paid and the rest of the money is used for repairing the Castle wall and maintaining the bridge.

Now that her children have—to her regret—left home, Mrs. Gringe has started the Café la Gringe. It has, however, not been well-reviewed in the influential *Egg-on-Toast Restaurant Guide*. Mrs. Gringe may still find herself washing more money than knives and forks.

THE North Gate

HOW TO GET THERE: From outside the Castle, head south from the One Way Bridge toward the Castle. From within the Castle, follow the streets North; it is well signposted.

WHO LIVES THERE: The Gringe family lives in the gatehouse. The Bridge Boy works there from sunrise to sunset.

WHY YOU'D GO THERE: To get into the Castle—and to get out again.

WHY YOU WOULDN'T: You might not want to pay the toll—in which case, you would have to go in through the South Gate just past the rubbish dump.

THE ABSOLUTELY TOP-SECRET SEVEN-YEAR DIARY OF LUCY GRINGE

Year One

SPRING

MONDAY. *Boring dance class today. Mum says I have to go. But WHY?*

TUESDAY. *Class yesterday not so bad. Met this boy called Simon. He's nice.*

MONDAY. *Asked Simon his name. He said Simon. I said (ha ha) I know that I mean what is your second name and he said Heap. I said you can't mean that and he said yes I do mean that what is the problem and I said my dad thinks you Heaps are nuts. But what I really meant was that I want to keep seeing Simon and I know that Dad will go crazy. What will I do?*

Year Two

SUMMER

SATURDAY. *Met Simon this afternoon at our secret place. It is across the One Way Bridge. No one knows. I love him.*

Year Five

WINTER

THURSDAY. *The Heaps have left! Everyone is talking about it,* **AND SI HAS GONE WITH THEM.** *I can't believe it! How could he go and not tell me?*

SUNDAY. *Woke up this morning before dawn. Thought it was raining as I heard pattering on the windows. But the rain was Si! He was throwing little stones at my window. How romantic is that? So I went downstairs really quietly as I knew that Dad would be up any minute. Si had such a big smile when he saw me! He asked me to marry him and I said yes yes YES! So we went to the Chapel and we waited until it was open and it was my dream come true. Except it didn't. It was horrible. There was a* CRASH *and the Custodian Guards rushed in. They took Si away even though he punched at least* **THREE** *of them and they brought me home. Mum and Dad went crazy. I have never heard such a racket. Now Dad has locked me in the attic because I told him I was going to rescue Simon and I didn't care what happened to me* SO THERE. *Mum and Dad are horrible. The Custodian Guards are horrible.* EVERYONE *is horrible. Except for Si. Oooooooooooooooooh.*

WHAT DAY IS IT? *I don't know. I don't care. I have a rat up here and it is my only friend. I am feeding it biscuits.*

ANOTHER BORING DAY. Mum came and tried to talk to me, but I ignored her. Was too busy embroidering my tunic to bother with HER. My only friend is my rat. He is called Stanley and he talks enough for anyone. Who needs stupid parents anyway?

SPRING

MONDAY. Dad said I can come out of the attic. Told him I liked the attic and I didn't want to SO THERE and he could just GO AWAY. So he left the door open and then as he was going he said something AWFUL. He said that Simon has disappeared in the Marshes and we won't ever see him again. I don't believe him. Dad is SO horrible. From now on I shall not call him Dad, I shall call him Father (which I know he hates).

Year Six

SUMMER

Had a huge fight with Mum on the drawbridge. And with Father too. Simon's little brother came and said that Si had kidnapped Princess Jenna. At first I was just so happy that Si is still alive! It has been so long since I heard anything. But why didn't he come and kidnap me? WHY? I am SO unhappy.

AUTUMN

TUESDAY. Princess Jenna came here today! She gave me a beautiful blue cloak and said that Simon had meant for me to have it. I didn't know what to say. I know all the bad stuff they have been saying about Si kidnapping Jenna and trying to kill Marcia and all that, but I don't believe it. Jenna wouldn't have come to see me if he had kidnapped her, would she? And she was really nice too.

My own
Lucy,

This cloak is for you.
I will be back soon and we will be
together at the top of the Tower.
I shall make you proud of me.

Wait for me.
Your only,
Simon.

Found this
in the cloak.
I am SO
happy!!!!!

AUTUMN

THURSDAY. *Where IS he? I have waited forever and he has still not come. I AM SO MAD. Have woven some ribbons.*

FRIDAY. *Had another argument with Father who told me to "stop mooning around like a sick ferret and do something." So I am GOING to do something. I am going to find Simon! I don't know where he is, but I figure the Port is a good place to start. I shall take the Outside Path tonight and then there is no chance of meeting ~~Dad~~ Father on his way to see silly old Silas Heap. Good-bye, horrible Castle!!!*

MONDAY. *Arrived at the Port in Nicko Heap's boat. The Heaps are okay really. Even Septimus is not a bad kid although he did say some rotten stuff about Simon. And Nicko reminds me so much of Si—something about the way he laughs. Am working at the Harbor and Dock Pie Shop for Maureen and Kevin. They are both really nice.*

FRIDAY. *Tons of rats here. Am sure one of them is that Message Rat I fed in the attic. I wonder if he knows where Si is?*

SATURDAY. *It IS Stanley. I am SURE he knows where Simon is! He keeps going on about it being "top secret," but I shall get him to tell me eventually. I have a motto now: "No One Says No to Lucy Gringe!"*

THE Message Rat Office
EAST GATE LOOKOUT TOWER

HOW TO GET THERE: Located in the East Gate Lookout Tower. Take the steps by the Manuscriptorium up to the path along the Wall and, keeping the Moat on your right, the tower is about a ten minute walk. When you can smell garbage, you are there.

WHO WORKS THERE: Stanley. No other rats are employed at present, but there are vacancies.

WHAT YOU'LL FIND THERE: A sign on the door that reads:

```
    RATS WANTED FOR MESSAGE RAT DUTIES
           NO EXPERIENCE NECESSARY
        FULL TRAINING WILL BE GIVEN
                 APPLY WITHIN
```

And another that reads:

```
               BEST RATES OF PAY
        WE PAY DOUBLE THE PORT RATE!
DON'T MISS OUT ON THIS WONDERFUL OPPURTUNITY!!
```

And one more that reads:

FREE FOOD!!!!!!

WHY YOU'D GO THERE: To send a message.

WHY YOU WOULDN'T: With only one rat on duty, the office may be closed while the rat is out on a message. Also if the one rat *is* in the office you may not want to listen to the rat's wide-ranging observations on Life, the Universe and Everything.

STANLEY: MY LIFE—A RAT'S RAMBLINGS

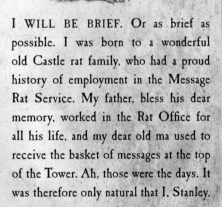

I WILL BE BRIEF. Or as brief as possible. I was born to a wonderful old Castle rat family, who had a proud history of employment in the Message Rat Service. My father, bless his dear memory, worked in the Rat Office for all his life, and my dear old ma used to receive the basket of messages at the top of the Tower. Ah, those were the days. It was therefore only natural that I, Stanley,

their pride and joy, should go into the Service—as it was known in the family.

I had not been long in the Service when I met my future wife, Dawnie, one summer's evening at my favorite rubbish bin. She emerged with gravy all over her nose and I was (unfortunately, as it turned out) smitten.

At Dawnie's insistence, we set up house together next door to her mother. The arrangement was not entirely successful. Dawnie's mother told my dear old ma, who was not well at the time, that she did not consider me good enough for her daughter. Not good, I hear you say—and how right you are.

The crisis point in my marriage came when I was kidnapped—or ratnapped—by Mad Jack. It was a nightmare. I was away for more than two months, and Dawnie's mother told her that I had done this deliberately to spite them. Well, I can think of much more pleasant things to do to spite someone than *that*.

My homecoming to the Castle was not good. After all I had been through, I was expecting a hero's welcome, but it was not to be. Dawnie had left and gone to live with her sister, Mabel. I was interrogated by the Rat Office and thrown into a disgusting little cage under the floor.

After I was released from imprisonment I spent some time recovering in the North Gate gatehouse under the care of the delightful Lucy Gringe. Not unnaturally, I am sure you will agree, I decided that I had had enough of the Message Rat Service.

Then one day, by the very same rubbish bin where I had first met Dawnie, I was approached by a shifty-looking rat and asked if I would like to join the Secret Rat Service. I accepted at once. It was my dream job.

My first Mission was one that I will never forget. I was dispatched to find the kidnapped Princess and return her to the Castle! How many rats have had that kind of responsibility entrusted to them? Not many, I can tell you. Those who know me well will know that I do not like to blow my own trumpet, but as a matter of record I have to say that I succeeded magnificently—there is no point pretending otherwise. Being a romantic at heart, I decided to try again with Dawnie.

Our reunion was not all it could have been. Dawnie's mother came over for supper *every* night. But the main problem was the RatStranglers—a bunch of thugs running a campaign to rid the Castle of rats. I wanted to go to the Port, but Dawnie would not leave her mother. However, one morning we discovered that her mother had legged it overnight and left us behind—so at last Dawnie agreed to go.

But fate was against us—as we crept out we were spotted by the RatStranglers. It was a terrifying chase and we only narrowly escaped by grabbing on to a departing dragon's tail.

It turned out that the dragon belonged to the Princess's brother, whom I had met before. I move in interesting circles, actually, and it does help at times. We were offered a ride on the dragon to the Port, but it was on this trip that the scales fell from my eyes and I saw Dawnie's true nature for the very first time. It was not a pretty sight and was the beginning of the end. Dawnie is now living in the Port near the pie shop. I hear she is even fatter.

But I am determined to be positive. Many good things have come out of this experience, and I am now considered to be, among other things, *a friend of royalty*. Sometimes I wonder what Dawnie would think of this, but deep down I know that Dawnie wouldn't really care. She has no soul.

Recently I have adopted four orphan ratlets, whom I found on the Outside Path one night.

I have also restarted the Message Rat Service and am hoping to find some staff soon. All applicants welcome. Free interview. But the ratlets are growing fast and if I don't find any staff, I will soon have some homegrown talent entering the Service. It will save on wages too.

All things work out in the end, don't they?

⊹ RULES ⊹

1. A message **MUST** be delivered no matter what.

2. A message must **ONLY** be delivered to the identified recipient.

3. A Message Rat **ALWAYS** travels undetected.

4. A Message Rat **NEVER** makes himself known to strangers.

5. A Message Rat may **NOT** refuse an assignment.

6. Message Rats carry messages **ONLY**. No parcels.

7. **ALL** conversations in the Rat Office are Highly Confidential.

REMEMBER: **NOTHING** STOPS A MESSAGE RAT!

Standard Message Form
to be used by ALL RATS

Await Command to speak. Wizards will use Speeke, Rattus Rattus. Non-Wizards use a variety of Commands, not all of them polite. But a Message Rat *never answers back* and *never deviates* from the Standard Message Form (SMF).

SMF is:

- *First, I have to ask: Is there anyone here answering to the name of* (INSERT NAME OF RECIPIENT)?

- Following recipient identifying him or herself correctly, deliver message in SMF:

- *I have come here to* deliver a message to (INSERT NAME OF RECIPIENT).

- *The message is sent* (INSERT DAY) *at* (INSERT TIME) *from* (INSERT NAME OF SENDER HERE AND, IF POSSIBLE, PLACE OF RESIDENCE).

- *Message begins:*

- Deliver Message VERBATIM. A Message Rat does not paraphrase, gabble, abbreviate or censor. At end of message sign off with:

- *Message ends.*

REMEMBER: A MESSAGE RAT IS PROFESSIONAL AT ALL TIMES.

Be proud of your Service.

Zone Pricing

ZONE 1: Inside the Castle wall

Outward Message only.................. 1 penny

Outward Message and wait for reply
   (MAXIMUM OF TEN MINUTES' WAIT) ...... 2 pence

Next day Return Message .... 3 pence

ZONE 2: Immediately outside the Castle wall as far as lower Farmlands, Infirmary. *Not* the Forest.

Outward Message only.................. 2 pence

Outward Message and wait for reply
   (MAXIMUM OF TEN MINUTES' WAIT) ...... 4 pence

Next day Return Message .... 6 pence

ZONE 3: The Port (BY SCHEDULED PORT BARGE ONLY). Positively *no* stop-offs for the Marram Marshes.

Outward Message only.................. 10 pence

Outward Message and wait for reply. (MAXIMUM OF TEN MINUTES' WAIT).................. 20 pence

Next day Return Message .... 30 pence

ZONES 4, 5, 6 AND 7: The Forest, the Sheeplands, the Badlands, Marram Marshes. *No* night messages accepted.

Outward Message only........Price on application

Outward Message and wait for reply (MAXIMUM OF FIFTEEN MINUTES' WAIT) .....Price on application

Next day Return Message ......Price on application

Please refer all requests for messages to these areas to the duty office rat. They are no longer accepted as a matter of course.

DISPATCHES FROM THE OLD
MESSAGE RAT OFFICE

MESSAGE STATUS:
RETURN MESSAGE

FROM: PRIVILEGE ACCOUNT HOLDER, ZELDA ZANUBA HEAP @ KEEPER'S COTTAGE, DRAGGEN ISLAND, MARRAM MARSHES

TO: PRINCESS JENNA @ THE PALACE, THE CASTLE

DEAR JENNA,

   I WAS SO PLEASED TO RECEIVE YOUR LETTER! BERT AND I ENJOYED READING IT VERY MUCH INDEED. I AM GETTING A REPLY STRAIGHT BACK TO YOU. EXCUSE ME IF IT IS A LITTLE RUSHED, BUT THE RAT WILL ONLY WAIT FOR FIFTEEN MINUTES. I DON'T KNOW WHAT THE MESSAGE RAT SERVICE IS COMING TO.

   I AM SO PLEASED THAT YOU AND YOUR PARENTS ARE ADJUSTING WELL TO LIFE IN THE PALACE. IT MUST SEEM VERY BIG AFTER YOUR COZY ROOM IN THE RAMBLINGS. I DO UNDERSTAND THAT YOU ARE UPSET THAT YOUR ROOM HAS BEEN EMPTIED WHILE YOU WERE AWAY AND I AM SO SORRY THEY TOOK YOUR TEDDY. BUT I AM SURE MR. TED WILL BE ALL RIGHT AND I REALLY DON'T THINK ANYONE WOULD HAVE THROWN HIM ON THE RUBBISH DUMP, WHATEVER THEY DID WITH EVERYTHING ELSE. YOU COULD ASK MARCIA TO DO A FIND—OR, ON SECOND THOUGHT, MAYBE NOT. BUT ONE DAY SEPTIMUS WILL BE ABLE TO DO ONE FOR YOU.

   AND IMAGINE YOU WANTING A PONY! I AM AFRAID I DON'T KNOW ANYTHING ABOUT PONIES, BUT I THINK YOUR FATHER KNOWS OF SOME GOOD STABLES IN THE FARMLANDS.

   I AM VERY MUCH LOOKING FORWARD TO YOUR VISIT AT MIDSUMMER DAY.

   ALL MY LOVE, AUNT ZELDA XXX

FROM: ALICE NETTLES
@ WAREHOUSE NUMBER
NINE, THE PORT

TO: ALTHER MELLA,
DECEASED @ THE
HOLE IN THE WALL
TAVERN

DEAREST ALTHER,

    I HAVE JUST HEARD THE WONDERFUL NEWS—THAT MURDERING
VILLAIN HAS FLED THE CASTLE ALONG WITH ALL HIS CRONIES. ABOUT
TIME TOO, ALTHOUGH OF COURSE IT IS FAR TOO LATE FOR SOME
PEOPLE. SO SAD WHAT HAS HAPPENED . . .

    WE HAD A TERRIBLE STORM HERE A COUPLE OF WEEKS AGO AND
PARTS OF THE PORT WERE FLOODED. ONE WAREHOUSE WAS BREACHED AND
THE ENTIRE STOCK OF BONDED GOODS WAS LOOTED—OR "RECLAIMED" BY
THE OWNER I SUSPECT.

    I HAVEN'T SEEN YOU FOR A WHILE AND I DO WONDER IF YOU HAD
SOMETHING TO DO WITH THE ABOVE EVENTS? DO TELL. I SHALL BE IN
THE BLUE ANCHOR ON FRIDAY AFTER WORK.

    YOURS FOREVER, ALICE XX

FROM: PRIVILEGE
ACCOUNT HOLDER
EXTRAORDINARY
WIZARD @ THE
WIZARD TOWER

TO: TERRY TARSAL
@ TARSAL'S FINE
BOOTS AND SHOES,
OFF WIZARD WAY

DEAR MR. TARSAL,

    PLEASE FINISH PREPARING MY NEW PAIR OF SHOES *AS SOON
AS POSSIBLE.* THIS IS A MATTER OF EXTREME URGENCY. MY NEW
APPRENTICE HAS MISTAKENLY TURNED MY PRESENT PAIR INTO HOBNAIL
BOOTS. WITH EVERLASTING MUD.

    I SHALL COLLECT THE NEW PAIR THIS AFTERNOON.

    REGARDS, MADAM MARCIA OVERSTRAND, EXTRAORDINARY WIZARD

FROM: TERRY TARSAL
@ TARSAL'S FINE
BOOTS AND SHOES,
OFF WIZARD WAY

TO: PRIVILEGE
ACCOUNT HOLDER
EXTRAORDINARY
WIZARD @ THE
WIZARD TOWER

DEAR MADAM,

    I REGRET WE ARE CLOSED TODAY FOR STOCK-TAKING.

    ASSURING YOU, MADAM, OF OUR BEST SERVICE, TERRY TARSAL,
MASTER BOOT AND SHOEMAKER

MESSAGE STATUS:
RETURN RETURN
MESSAGE
URGENT

FROM: PRIVILEGE
ACCOUNT HOLDER
EXTRAORDINARY
WIZARD @ THE
WIZARD TOWER

TO: TERRY TARSAL
@ TARSAL'S FINE
BOOTS AND SHOES,
OFF WIZARD WAY

DEAR MR. TARSAL,

    IF THIS RAT REACHES YOU BEFORE I DO, YOU WILL BE FORTUNATE.
I SHALL BE ALONG TO COLLECT MY SHOES FORTHWITH.

    MADAM MARCIA OVERSTRAND, EXTRAORDINARY WIZARD

MESSAGE STATUS:
OUTWARD MESSAGE.
MESSAGE UNABLE TO BE
DELIVERED. INCORRECT/
INEXACT ADDRESS.
RETURN FEE INCURRED.

FROM: LUCY GRINGE
@ NORTH GATE
GATEHOUSE

TO: SIMON HEAP
@ THE BADLANDS

DEAREST SIMON,

    I AM LOST WITHOUT YOU. I WILL WAIT ON THE QUAY EVERY
EVENING UNTIL YOU ARRIVE. I LOVE YOU.

    YOURS FOREVER, LUCY XXXXXXXXXXXXXXXXXXXXXXX

MESSAGE STATUS:
OUTWARD MESSAGE

FROM: PRIVILEGE
ACCOUNT HOLDER,
EXTRAORDINARY
WIZARD @ THE
WIZARD TOWER

TO: PRIVILEGE
ACCOUNT HOLDER,
ZELDA ZANUBA HEAP
@ KEEPER'S COTTAGE,
DRAGGEN ISLAND,
MARRAM MARSHES

MY DEAR ZELDA,

    THAT IS *NOT* MY TOOTHBRUSH! I HAVE RETURNED IT TO YOU FOUR
TIMES NOW AND I GIVE UP. I WILL DONATE IT TO THE ASYLUM FOR
DISTRESSED PERSONS. I AM SURE THEY WILL BE PLEASED TO HAVE IT.

    REGARDS, MARCIA OVERSTRAND, EXTRAORDINARY WIZARD

P.S. SEPTIMUS HAS REQUESTED YOU TO SEND HIM A CABBAGE SANDWICH.
I TOLD HIM THAT GIVEN THE INEFFICIENCY OF THE RIVER POST AND
PACKET COMPANY IT WOULD BE STALE BY THE TIME IT ARRIVED, BUT
HE SAYS THE SANDWICHES TASTE EVEN BETTER STALE. PLEASE NOTE
THAT THE PASSING-ON OF THIS MESSAGE DOES NOT INDICATE APPROVAL.

FROM: PRIVILEGE ACCOUNT HOLDER, ZELDA ZANUBA HEAP @ KEEPER'S COTTAGE, DRAGGEN ISLAND, MARRAM MARSHES

TO: PRIVILEGE ACCOUNT HOLDER, EXTRAORDINARY WIZARD @ THE WIZARD TOWER

DELIVERY 7 ZONE

DEAR MARCIA,

PLEASE DO NOT DISTRESS YOURSELF ABOUT YOUR TOOTHBRUSH. I QUITE UNDERSTAND. I WOULD BE EMBARRASSED TOO.

YOURS, ZELDA

DELIVERY 7 ZONE

FROM: PRIVILEGE ACCOUNT HOLDER, ZELDA ZANUBA HEAP @ KEEPER'S COTTAGE, DRAGGEN ISLAND, MARRAM MARSHES

TO: SEPTIMUS HEAP, EXTRAORDINARY APPRENTICE @ THE WIZARD TOWER

DEAREST SEPTIMUS,

JUST TO LET YOU KNOW, I WILL SEND THE REQUESTED CABBAGE SANDWICH VIA THE RIVER POST AND PACKET COMPANY. I BELIEVE THEIR ESTIMATED DELIVERY TIME IS TEN DAYS. IT SHOULD BE JUST RIGHT BY THEN!

I DO HOPE ALL IS GOING WELL FOR YOU AT THE WIZARD TOWER. YOU ARE A VERY BRAVE BOY. DON'T WORK TOO HARD. I THINK OF YOU OFTEN.

ALL MY LOVE, AUNT ZELDA XXX

FROM: PRIVILEGE ACCOUNT HOLDER, ZELDA ZANUBA HEAP @ KEEPER'S COTTAGE, DRAGGEN ISLAND, MARRAM MARSHES

TO: SARAH HEAP @ THE PALACE, THE CASTLE

DELIVERY 7 ZONE

DEAREST SARAH,

THIS IS A TRULY TERRIBLE BUSINESS WITH NICKO. IT IS PROBABLY OF LITTLE COMFORT TO YOU, BUT ALTHOUGH UNFORTUNATELY I CANNOT TELL YOU THAT I HAVE SENSED HIS PRESENCE ANYWHERE, I DO FEEL CERTAIN HE IS NOT DEAD. AS YOU REQUESTED, I ATTEMPTED A SCRYING AT THE FULL MOON AND SAW NOTHING BUT WHITE. IT WAS MOST ODD. I DID WONDER AFTERWARD IF I WAS SEEING A WHITE MIST OR SNOW, BUT THAT IS OF LITTLE USE NOW. IT IS A CONUNDRUM. IT IS AS THOUGH HE IS HERE AND YET NOT HERE. ALIVE AND YET NOT— NO NO, I WILL NOT GO ON. THE TRUTH OF IT IS, SARAH DEAR, I HAVE NO ANSWERS.

PLEASE SEND MY LOVE TO JENNA AND SEPTIMUS, AND TO POOR SILAS.

WITH LOVE, AUNT ZELDA XXX

THE EGG-ON-TOAST RESTAURANT GUIDE
by G. M. Toast

⚜ Eating Outside the Castle ⚜

Sally Mullin's Tea and Ale house

★★★★☆

PROPRIETOR: Miss Sally Mullin.
LOCATION: A new wooden building on the pontoon just above the Quay. Good river views are somewhat spoiled by the closeness of the amenity to the rubbish dump.
SERVICE: Good. Order at the counter and Sally or her assistant will bring it to you.

SPECIALTIES: Sally Mullin's renowned barley cake and Springo Special Ale. The barley cake is a little heavy for some tastes and THE EGG-ON-TOAST RESTAURANT GUIDE advises that you treat the Springo Special Ale with caution.
MENU: Many varieties of barley cake, homemade hot pot, small selection of pies, baked potatoes, apple buns and an assortment of hot chocolate drinks and ales.
WE ATE: Barley cake and hot pot. My assistant had the Springo Special after being offered sausage pie.
COMMENTS: Very enjoyable. Miss Mullin can be a little talkative.

The Egg Box

★★★

PROPRIETOR: Ava Poltava.

LOCATION: Half a mile past the Grateful Turbot you will find a stone hut at the gate of the Chicken Farm—the first farm on the way to the Farmlands. Has yellow-and-white-striped awning on sunny days.

SERVICE: Friendly, although a little slow at chicken-feeding times.

SPECIALTIES: Soft poached egg in a freshly baked bun.

MENU: Anything to do with eggs, including one hundred varieties of omelette.

WE ATE: Eggy bread washed down with a glass of eggnog.

COMMENTS: Fine, as long as you like eggs and don't mind the occasional peck.

The Grateful Turbot Tavern

★★☆☆☆

PROPRIETOR: Mr. Dan T. Specter and Mrs. P. Geist.

LOCATION: Just across the One Way Bridge on the other side of the river.

SERVICE: A little gloomy but reasonably efficient.

SPECIALTIES: None.

MENU: Basic food.

WE ATE: Obviously not the sausages. Bean dumplings with cabbage and fish.

COMMENTS: The fish was dubious and the authors of THE EGG-ON-TOAST RESTAURANT GUIDE were unwell that night. The inn had a very strange atmosphere. It felt particularly chilly beside the fire.

INDEX

Visit www.septimusheap.com for games,
fun, and **Magyk**!

Collect character trading cards
Play Septimus Heap games
Learn **Magykal** Spells

Read the novels in the Septimus Heap series

Septimus Heap
✢ Book Five ✢
Syren
Available Fall 2009